POLLEN

stories

DAVID WAGSTAFF

QUIET LION PRESS
Portland, Oregon

Pollen
©2024 David Wagstaff

Author photo by Sofia Angelina
Cover photo by Heidi Kirkpatrick
Cover and book design by Brian Hamilton & Lyndsay Henn

ISBN 1-882550-57-9

FIRST EDITION

10 9 8 7 6 5 4 3 2 1

QUIET LION PRESS
7215 sw LaView Drive
Portland, Oregon 97219

Eroticism is a realm stalked by ghosts.
It is the place beyond the pale,
both cursed and enchanted.
—CAMILLE PAGLIA

CONTENTS

BEYOND THE PALE

I FIRST GLIMPSED the haunted realm one rainy Sunday morning in 1956 as I sang "Come to the Church in the Wildwood" with twenty other second graders at the Roanoke Island Methodist Church. We were directed in song by our Sunday school teacher, Miss Connie, a recent high-school graduate (she showed us her diploma). Miss Connie loved Jesus without measure. I loved Miss Connie without measure. I lived for the moments when she knelt by my chair, pulled me close, and kissed my temple with soft lips as she praised my skill with crayons. She loved all of God's children, but I knew I was one of her favorites, owing to my ability to recite scripture on command. "You children are so important to Jesus," she would tell us, beaming with evangelical sweetness. Given my coloring and reciting talents, I was sure I was especially important to Jesus.

On this particular Sunday, the spring rain poured in sheets beyond the chapel window as Miss Connie directed "Church in the Wildwood" on her tiptoes, using a pencil for a baton. She was accompanied by the church's enormous pianist, Mrs. Blanchard, who, with sheet music spread wide before her, pounded the keys with fat-jiggling determination. Her immense breasts arched from beneath her bejeweled neck like the backs of albino porpoises diving into the dark sea of her frock, her lips pursed in song and her eyes heavy lidded with religious ecstasy as the trill of our untrained voices rose to heaven:

> *Oh come, come, come to the church in the Wildwood*
> *Oh come to the church in the dale*

Miss Connie mouthed the words for us as Mrs. Blanchard charged ahead, her own warbling soprano joining the mess we made of the simple melody:

> *There's a church in the valley by the wildwood*
> *No lovelier spot in the dale*
> *No place is so dear to my childhood*
> *As the little brown church in the vale*

Suddenly, sun burst through the clouds and transformed the droplet-dappled windowpanes into sheets of diamonds, bathing us in radiance. Miss Connie was backlit by this glory, her hair a living tangle of gossamer baby snakes, the thin fabric of her summer dress all but vanishing in heaven's light.

> *Come to the church in the wildwood*
> *Oh, come to the church in the dale*
> *No spot is so dear to my childhood*
> *As the little brown church in the vale*

My mouth wide with song, I saw with divine clarity the defiant curve of Miss Connie's breasts and the smooth naked flesh-wood of her slender trunk flowing downward into the rounding of her hips.

How sweet on a clear, Sabbath morning
To list to the clear ringing bell
Its tones so sweetly are calling
Oh, come to the church in the vale

Now Miss Connie turned to direct the tiny sopranos to my left. She bent slightly at the waist, bobbing her head to encourage them, her breasts bouncing with soft animal elasticity to the rhythm of the refrain:

Oh come, come, come, to the church in the wildwood
Oh come to the church in the dale

The light grew blinding and I turned away. My eyes fell on our preacher's daughter, Damine, and she became engulfed in my enchantment by divine transubstantiation.

There, close by the church in the valley
Lies one that I loved so well
She sleeps, sweetly sleeps, 'neath the willow
Disturb not her rest in the vale

Damine held her head high, her posture flawless, her mouth moving in magic, as if every voice in the room passed through her lips.

I stopped singing, able only to stare, drowning in the pounding piano and the blondness of heaven, my senses electrified by the prisms of religious revelation. Damine's angelic singing profile, her amber-lit skin, and the sun-naked body of our Sunday school teacher were imprinted forever on the wet panes of my memory by the will of God.

Oh come, come, come, to the church in the wildwood
Oh come to the church in the dale

The clouds closed and heaven retreated. The raindrops on the windowpanes lost their diamond souls. Miss Connie's angelic nudity faded and she stood before us—a mortal teenager in the sheath of her plain dress.

Oh come, come, come, to the church in the wildwood
Oh come to the church in the dale

The next day at school, I mustered the courage to write Damine a note in the best second-grade protocol: "Dear Damine, I love you. Do you love me?" Beneath this I drew two boxes—one labeled YES and the other NO. I signed my name with trembling hands and gave it to her best friend for delivery. It was swiftly returned and I opened it carefully, my heart thundering. Here was my Destiny.

She had inscribed a neat x in the YES box. At the bottom of the page she had written in her own neat script: "Would you die for me?" There were two boxes labeled for my reply.

By the time school ended for the year, Damine and I were "going steady" and we had the whole summer ahead of us to explore our new love in that distant Land of Time of the 1950s before adults took over childhood. Called home by mothers' voices for lunch and dinner, we children owned the chasm of time between meals: board games on the back porch, imaginary battles, unsupervised baseball, the trapping of wild amphibians, or, in the case of Damine and me, trips to the docks to watch the boats, ice cream cones from Hubbie's store, and walks in the woods.

One day, as we cut through the woods to get ice cream, we came across a board nailed horizontally to a tree three feet off the ground.

"Looks like someone was gonna build a ladder up this tree," I said.

"No," Damine replied, "it's a cross. Somebody was

praying here."

"People don't pray in the woods."

"They built a cross, didn't they?"

She walked around the tree. The crosspiece was at the level of her shoulders. She touched it fondly.

"Have you been saved?" she inquired.

I had not. My family was reserved. We were from Ohio and sat primly in the rear of the church when the congregation, led by Rev. Marcus, Damine's father, fell to speaking in tongues and getting saved. But I was a believer—I had Miss Connie to thank for that.

"Well, I've been saved," she said. "I can do anything I want and be forgiven."

"You could kill someone?"

"I wouldn't, but I could. I could take off all my clothes right here and God would forgive me. If you took yours off you would burn in hell."

"I dare you to."

She did. Then she stood against the tree, cruciform, with the back of her arms pressed against the cross board. "This is how Jesus died for our sins." She let her head fall to one side and closed her eyes, motionless, her mouth slightly open to mimic the pain of crucifixion. Again I felt the presence of God.

The exercise complete, she dropped her arms and pointed to the tiny heap of her clothes: shorts, white underwear, and a T-shirt. I handed them to her.

"Turn around while I get dressed," she said.

When we were nearly out of the woods she said, "Did you look at me when I was naked?"

"You were right in front of me."

"That was a sin. You should get saved. Then God will forgive you."

"Don't tell me what to do all the time."

"You shouldn't have checked the box then."

"What box?"

"The one that said 'Would you die for me?' If you would die for me, then you should get saved for me."

She took my hand and we walked in silence, into the unknown and the promise of ice cream.

OF MEG AND MEN

THERE WERE TWO framed black-and-white pictures on the mantle above the fireplace in our house. One was the formal portrait of my parents on their wedding day, the other was of my father accepting a trophy from General Thurmond Houser, my dad having just knocked out his opponent in the second round to win the U.S. Army welterweight title in 1942. The other men in the ring stand with their hands behind their backs, in deference to Houser's rank. My father, six inches taller than the general, accepts the trophy with one hand as he shakes the general's hand with the other. On the general's face is an unmistakable look of respect. On my father's face is the same broad, easy smile he wore in the wedding photo.

In 1945, when the war ended, he "spared himself the boredom of college," as he put it, and boxed professionally for two years. He had a respectable record of twenty-two wins and seven losses, but quit boxing when my mother made it a condition for marriage. My father entered the unlikely profession of salesman in my grandfather's furniture store. At first, his father-in-law had "deep doubts about this Palooka." Within a year, however, he was won over by a steep climb in sales. "Natural-born salesman," Grandpa claimed, and so built what amounted to a shrine in one corner of the showroom: the trophy from the Army title, framed pictures and news clippings from my father's boxing career that included one titled "Does He Have What It Takes To Be The Next Champ?" No one would ever know, but it was clear he had the right footwork and killer instinct to sell the hell out of furniture.

He was a smart man, my father—not necessarily intelligent or literate, but quick and instinctive about everything. For example, no one could lie to him. He looked at you and knew. If I offered my mother a piece of fiction as to why my brother and I came home late from school, her litmus test was simple: "Do you want to tell that story to your father?" I never saw anyone beat him at chess, though he was not a regular player. It was a kind of parlor trick to him. My mother's brothers were big chess players, but once he learned how to play they just couldn't whip him. "It's a game of anticipation," he explained to them. "You just look at the board and see what's ahead. Then when your opponent throws a punch, you duck and counter." My uncles were both college graduates, a teacher and a civil engineer, and they'd had their doubts about my mother marrying a pugilist. As my mother told it, they made snide remarks to his face about his lack of education and that he never read the paper beyond the sports page and the comics. No doubt they taught him to play chess to continue the fun—their mistake.

My earliest clear memory of my father is his soothing baritone as he hovered above me. "The power of the punch comes from shifting your weight." He held my wrists, moving my body to and fro, back and forth, as he threw the punch with my tiny hand buried inside the huge red boxing glove. It worked so perfectly when he guided me and not so well when he did not. I must have been five or so.

My brother Devon, eleven months younger than me, was my training partner. In the center of the living room, wearing the huge, over-padded gloves, we pawed at each other like two tiger kittens, much to my father's delight as he coached us from the couch. I suspect that even as I lay in my crib when I was a baby, he was already moving my little arms in tiny combinations. "Jab, jab, cross. That's it."

Soon the sessions moved to our double-car garage, where my father had everything we needed to learn the sweet science: heavy bag, speed bags, jump ropes, and a variety of gloves. In the center lay a large square mat for sparring. This is where my father trained for fights he no longer had—and where he trained his sons.

We had a speed bag mounted three feet off the floor; I enjoyed learning the rhythm that kept the bag going. And I liked the heavy bag, too, once I'd begun to master the art of shifting my weight to get maximum impact. But there was one thing I didn't like: jumping rope. In fact, I hated it, so I worked up my courage one day and told my father I didn't want to jump rope anymore. He said, "That's not your decision to make, son."

I had no opportunity to use what he taught me until I was in the first grade. Our teacher had provided my art partner and me with a glob of white paste so we might stick Christmas shapes onto sheets of green and red construction paper, but through poor workmanship, the chunky, snot-nosed boy sitting across the table from us had squandered his own paste and snatched ours. My partner was a tiny, shy Mexican girl with pierced ears, and her huge brown eyes brimmed with tears. She took the pasting project seriously, her delicate brown fingers patting each shape carefully into place. Watching her cry, a throbbing panic overtook me. I stood, pushed in my chair, walked around the table and delivered a solid punch to the back of glue thief's head. He sat stunned for a few seconds with a thick glob of stolen paste on his finger, then broke down crying himself, rubbing the back of his head. My pretty partner laughed through her tears and I was taken to the principal.

The principal was the tallest woman I'd ever seen, and perhaps the skinniest. I explained the glue theft—he had made my partner cry, he was not a gentleman.

"He was not a gentleman? So you smacked him?" She sneered imperiously down at me, picked up the phone, and called my mother, who came to pick me up.

The next day my father sat in his suit across from the principal, the woman all students feared, and she did not look so frightening. I don't remember what he said to her, but I'd heard that tone before when he was selling couches and refrigerators. I do remember her smiling at him when she recalled my saying that I hit the boy because he'd made a little girl cry and was not a gentleman.

"You don't hear that word often from the mouth of a first-grader," she said. "You must be a good father."

"What did you learn from this?" my father asked me after the meeting. I sat across from him, eating a grilled cheese sandwich at a diner owned by one of his friends.

"Not to hit people?"

"There is a time and place to hit people," my father said, "and don't ever let people tell you different. But you chose the wrong time, and timing is everything. In war and sales, timing is everything." He smiled at the waitress and she smiled back. "Learn from this. In life, someone is always going to be going after your glue and women are always going to be crying for one reason or another. You have to hit some people, and you're gonna get hit yourself from time to time. There's no other way, and there's nothing like getting tagged on the chin to teach you to keep your guard up." He smiled down at me and patted me on the back. "Use this. Learn."

I remembered his advice and was never suspended for fighting again, though I fought more or less continuously; the town and time where I grew up ordained it. Toughness and the willingness to fight were social and moral virtues. Everyone knew who could whip whom in each grade and, since I was a trained fighter, I was always at the top of the hierarchy in my year. Often, I moved up a few divisions, much like a welterweight fighting a middleweight. In the fourth grade, I could take the fifth- and sixth-grade badasses, as well, but I never fought at school. In war and sales, timing is everything. I met challengers off school grounds and away from houses where someone might call the police.

My father congratulated me on my wisdom and I continued to train in the garage with the speed bag, the heavy bag, and punching my father's hands as he moved around the garage giving me instruction. He advised against anger. "When you are mad, you make mistakes. Just watch him," he'd say. "Talk to him a little. Distract him."

And so, as I advanced through second, third, fourth and fifth grade, I developed a variety of insults to distract my opponents before and during the fight. I had a litany of slanders about my opponents' looks, physiques, and unstylish clothes. By the time I was thirteen, the scope of my insults had expanded to include my opponents' mothers and their sexual activities with dogs. This particular tactic was especially effective in drawing out the reluctant combatant; working-class folks are sensitive to the disrespect of mothers. These angry young men of honor would take their first wild swing and I'd go to work. The fights were usually over quickly. Afterward, I apologized about the mother talk and, with the hierarchy established or solidified, we usually became friends. I suffered defeats only to much older guys who could wrestle my eighty pounds to the ground and twist my arm or bang my head on the ground until I gave up.

But I was respected. Devon had given up on boxing and

focused, as early as the second grade, on girls and girls alone. For this reason, he was popular with girls and unpopular—well, hated—by boys. From time to time, he was accosted or threatened and I would have to take care of it. Usually the perpetrator didn't realize I was his brother, and when this came to light, Devon received a quick apology and it was over. This was the way I preferred it; I didn't like beating up kids in Devon's grade as they were a year younger.

My mother was Devon's accomplice in romance—wrapping presents for Devon to take to his latest interest on her birthday or shining his shoes so he could make a good impression. He belonged to my mother and I to my father, and sometimes they'd criticize each other's parenting in drawn-out debates behind their locked bedroom door that ended with my mother sobbing and my father leaving for the evening without putting on his tie.

He'd come home when the bars closed and we would hear the song of their moaning reunion through the walls. My mother would celebrate the reconciliation with a big breakfast and extra coffee for my father, who sat with bloodshot eyes and told us we were both fine young men before leaving to sell furniture.

Our lives were clean and simple.

The year I was in the seventh grade, the Kolbeonsons moved in across the street one day in January when the town was a foot deep in rare snow and the schools had been closed in fear of bus accidents on the slick highways. The Kolbeonsons arrived not in a moving van but in a series of pickup trucks and hitch-drawn trailers pulled by rattling, smoky cars driven by an assortment of red-haired people. This led my mother to conclude that they were of Irish extraction. She was incorrect—they would later claim to be Spanish, though none of them spoke Spanish.

"Dirt poor," my father exclaimed, gazing from our front

window as a horde of redheads of all ages dragged open-topped boxes and unmatched furniture across the frozen white yard and into the drab, hopeless-looking house across the street. He took a deep drag on his Camel and shook his head. "I hate the smell of poverty." He put on his overcoat and brown leather gloves. "I'm going to go say hello."

Collar up against the cold, he advanced, ghostlike, through the snow to their curb, but before he could cross the yard to their door a fat man in a motorcycle jacket strode out as if to block his path. My mother, brother and I stood at the window watching through the silence of floating snowflakes. They talked for a minute, and then my father extended his hand. The arm in the leather jacket stayed at his side and there was a long moment of silence. Neither moved, though my father's gloved hand remained extended. The man said something, nodded in the direction of our house, and walked away.

We heard, across the muffled distance, my father's raised voice. The man turned and came at my father, his faced screwed up with anger, his belly jiggling in the unclosable gap between his faded Levis and the leather jacket. My father stood still in his camel-hair overcoat, then raised his left arm at the last moment to block the man's awkward overhand right. Then, stepping forward with his left foot, he shifted his weight at exactly the correct moment, just as he'd taught me, and delivered a right cross that dropped his moving target in the snow as if he'd run into an invisible wall of stone. The man lay still in the snow.

"Oh, my God," my mother whispered.

My father stooped over his prey and called out to the red-headed movers who had stopped their work and were staring at this strange scene. As my father pulled the fat man to his feet, three other men crossed the yard. One of them took the wobbly fellow into the house while my father stood talking to the other two. He was at ease, gesturing as I'd seen him do in the furniture store: gently, first with his left and then with his right, slow open-palmed moves, threatless and soothing. There was no hint in his stature or movement that he'd just rendered one of them unconscious. The men listened, looking occasionally at one another. Finally, one of the men extended his hand and my father shook it, then offered his hand to the other. One of them called up at the house and a thin, stooped woman without a coat came out and crossed the trampled snow, clutching her arms against the cold. She was introduced to my father and the two men seemed to give her some kind of instructions before sending her back to the house. They all shook hands again and parted.

My father stomped his shoes on the front porch. He stepped inside with the preoccupied expression he often wore when he came home from work. He seemed to be surprised we were there.

"What was that all about?" my mother asked. He took off his coat and hung it carefully in the front hall closet.

"Every family has a weird uncle, and I was unlucky enough to meet him right off the bat."

"I think he was the unlucky one." She smiled up at him, one hand at her heart, forever dispelling from my mind the myth that women abhor the violence of men. Later we heard them in their room; it sounded like reconciliation, though the fight had not been between them.

The school secretary brought Meg Kolbeonson into our class just before lunch. She hardly looked like a girl—scrawny and redheaded like her mother and brothers, she wore jeans, a t-shirt, and a thin denim jacket with the collar up. She beat the hell out of a fifth-grade boy after school. He'd made the mistake of asking if she was a boy or a girl. Someone finally pulled her off him and she took a swing at that guy, too. Devon reported all this to me in a hushed voice. He was awed. "She can fight, I swear to God."

"But she *is* a girl, right?"

"Well, her name is Megan. What do you think? Of course she's a girl. I bet you she's going to wanna fight you."

"Why would she want to fight me? I'm not going to insult her."

"No, she's gonna want to prove something. I can tell."

He was right. The word came around that she thought she could take me and that I looked like a chickenshit. Maybe she wanted revenge for my father knocking out her weird uncle in the snow. I considered asking my father what to do, and then regretted not having done so when I stood face-to-face with her on the path across the field behind our housing tract. She stood with her feet apart, sneering up at me.

"So are you gonna fight or not?" She had the voice of a girl, but spoke like a boy.

"I don't fight girls."

"Maybe you are a girl. Are you a girl? I heard you were a badass, but look at you, afraid to fight a girl littler than you." She shoved me hard and I landed on my ass. She may have sounded like a girl, but she shoved like a boy—a strong boy. I stood, backed up, and looked around. Everyone was waiting.

"No. I don't fight girls."

She moved to Devon. "What are you lookin' at?"

"Nothing," he said, and she punched him in the face. Caught off guard, he staggered back and covered it with his hands. She kicked him in the stomach and he curled forward, blood now running through his fingers. Enough was enough.

I came up on her and she swung with the same punch as her weird uncle. I blocked it with my left forearm and hit her in the forehead with a right cross. The left came again and caught me just above the ear. I hit her in the ribs and they gave. I pushed her away with my left forearm. I knew the rib shot hurt her, but she leapt on me like a cat—her legs were around my waist and she scratched the back of my neck with both hands, yet she was so light we didn't go down.

I didn't want to wrestle her. Even in my undeveloped pubescent sense of the world, I knew wrestling would cross a line. She bit my arm through my coat and I knew I had to hurt her to end it. I threw a right hook as hard as I could to the side of her head, then another, and another. She slid off me into the dirt and dove at my legs. I hit her hard with my fist like a hammer on the middle of her back.

She froze for a moment and then coughed. She knelt in front of me gasping and I was horrified that I had really hurt her.

"Are you all right?" I said. I knelt beside her. "I didn't mean to hit you so hard."

She caught her breath and tried to stand up, reaching around and pressing with her hand where the hammer fist had caught her. "My brothers hit me harder than that," she said, but she was done.

She straightened up and looked at me, the side of her face red and swollen.

"Okay, you kicked my ass," she said. "You won." She got up and walked slowly down the path toward home.

Devon and I trailed behind her. His nose was no longer bleeding but there was blood smeared on his face and caked in his nostrils.

I watched her walking ahead of us. There wasn't a trace of girl in her stride. From behind, she was a boy, her collar up against the cold and her hair shorter than Devon's. We caught up with her.

"Where did you move from?" I asked.

"Florida. It's a lot warmer there."

"Too cold for you here?"

"No," she said, glancing over at me for a second, "I like the way the cold smells."

"You're pretty tough," I ventured. "My ear is ringing from that left."

"I don't remember which hand I hit you with."

"It was a roundhouse left."

She laughed. "You have names for punches?"

"My father was a boxer. He taught us how to fight."

"My parents are divorced," she offered. "Thank God. My dad's an asshole."

I had no response and we'd reached home. She paused on the sidewalk and looked at our house. "You guys rich?"

"I don't think so," Devon replied.

"Looks like it," she said and walked away.

"Bye," Devon said, but she didn't respond in kind.

The next day Meg and one of her brothers were waiting for me in the field. He was twice my size, red-headed, and smoking a cigarette. The kids we were walking with fell away as we approached. My heart pounded. This guy was huge and he looked plain mean. He stepped out and blocked my path. "This him?" he asked Meg.

"Yep."

"I hear you beat the shit out of my little sister."

"She wanted to fight."

"You fight girls? Well, I ain't a girl. Fight me." He flicked the cigarette at me and it sailed by my face.

"Do you want me to go get Dad?" Devon said.

"No." I handed Devon my books.

"Ok, come on," I said. "What? You think I'm afraid of you? Oh wow, he can smoke a cigarette. I'm shaking. Come on. What are you, like thirty or something?"

"I'm fifteen, you little prick."

I put up my fists and started moving to the left. He came at me and I just kept moving away. His hands were low, but I couldn't take advantage of it. His arms were too long. He continued to come at me and I kept moving back and to my left.

"Come on, you little shit, come on," he said, "Why are you backing away? Is this what daddy taught you? Is this how you fight out here in Bum Fuck Egypt?" Then he ran at me.

I dodged, but he grabbed my jacket and flung me to the ground. Then he was on top of me and the punches were all over my head and shoulders—I couldn't scramble away. I held my arms in front of my face and rolled face down in the dirt, but he kept pounding me. "Okay!" I yelled. "You win!" I was hurt.

"Yeah? You gonna apologize for beating up my sister, you little shit?"

"Yeah, I'm sorry. I'm sorry."

He got off and stood over me. "Don't think you're better than us," he said, "because you're not. You bleed like everybody else and your shit stinks just like everyone else. Leave my sister alone." He paused, looking around at the loose crowd, and lit another cigarette. "Let's go, Meg."

"I'm gonna walk with them," Meg said.

"Suit yourself." He walked off and I got up.

"You okay?" she asked.

"Do I look okay?" I dusted myself off. I was going to have lumps on my head, and my pants were torn.

The others moved on. This was going to be all over school.

"What do you care how I am? You pick a fight with me, and then have your big brother kick my ass. What did I do to you? Nothing. Nothing. And now you say you're going to walk with us? Are you crazy?"

"I had to pay you back. Besides, Toby found out what happened. He's got to stick up for his sister, don't he? You stuck up for your brother."

I walked off and she and Devon followed. I heard them talking quietly behind me. When we reached the house she said goodbye to Devon and crossed the street. We watched her go into the dilapidated house that had gone unpainted so long it was the color of the lawnless lot on which it sat.

"I think she likes you," Devon said.

"Oh yeah, love at first fight."

"Now that was a good one," Devon said. "Love at first fight. Come on, I'll cover for you while you hide those torn pants."

Again, Devon was right. Meg liked me, but not in the way I had ever been liked by a female before or since. She simply wanted to hang out with me and be friends. And so she did.

By summer, we were doing everything together. On hot summer days, when waves of heat rose from the streets, we swam at the public pool and hiked in the foothills. We also went to the park and picked fights. She was hard to beat because she never quit and everything about her was hard. Her small, chaffed hands were little cannonballs and she threw combinations. She was left-handed and liked to throw two left hooks and then a right. No one ever saw those hooks coming. I mean, who expects a girl of eighty-five pounds to throw a hard left hook, follow it up with another and step through with a right? She fought boys twenty pounds heavier and six inches taller.

Sometimes, much older guys came looking for us and we'd have to cool it for a while. Still, wherever we went, we were looking for a fight. It wasn't malicious, it was just what some of us did in the early sixties in our town. We weren't bullies—we didn't pick on people who didn't want to fight. We just let it be known one way or another that we were ready if someone else was ready.

Afterwards, we would nurse our wounds and analyze what had gone right or wrong. There were times when we got our asses kicked, but they were rare. There were also times when we had to get Toby or one of her other brothers to protect us from the older guys. By this time, the Kolbeonson brothers had a reputation, so everyone knew we had serious backup.

We also played a lot of baseball. I played Little League

the first year we were friends and Pony League the second. Meg went to all the games. I was a pitcher and Meg caught me for hours on our front lawn as I developed and practiced my pitches. My father worked long hours in the summer, but some evenings he worked out in the garage on the heavy bag with Devon and me. Meg came in to watch, but would never participate, even when my father invited her. She was embarrassed not to be a boy, I think, and called him "sir."

Meg asked about him when we were walking the streets late one night, stealing cigarettes out of unlocked cars. We'd started smoking together. She was curious about his boxing career and whether he beat us. "But what if you do something really bad, something that really pisses him off?"

"I've never seen him really pissed off," I told her. "He just isn't that way. He and my mom argue, but he would never hit one of his own family."

"Well, he sure kicked my uncle Leroy's ass. Leroy ain't been to our house since. Which is okay by me, 'cause he's a pervert."

On the night we graduated from eighth grade, Meg's brother Carl bought us two six-packs of Reingold beer and we got drunk with Devon, sitting in the field. After three or four beers, we staggered around like idiots in the moonlight. Out of the blue, she tackled me and climbed on top of me.

"You're the best friend I ever had in my life," she said, "and I ain't just sayin' that 'cause I'm drunk." She looked me dead in the eye. "We gotta stick together."

"We will," I said.

Half an hour later, we were on our hands and knees vomiting. Devon laughed at us. My brother was always a step ahead of the game. He drank enough to get drunk, but Meg and I had to take it too far.

A week later, my family went down to the Gulf of Mexico on vacation. We stayed at my aunt's house and went to the movies every night. My mother loved movies. Afterwards, my parents talked about the films for hours. Watching them, I saw how much my father loved my mother. He was gentle and agreeable, always giving in to her interpretation of the movie.

"Well, I think you're right," he'd say. "You have a deeper understanding of these things than I do. I'm just lucky to be married to such an intelligent woman."

My mother would glow. It sounds corny now, remembering how he wooed her long after they were married, how he was always a gentleman, sipping his martini on my aunt's patio and talking with his wife about some boring movie we'd seen. I know now, after being married myself, what a rare talent he had. Charm is genius, but the capability to maintain that genius after you've been flossing next to someone for twelve years is true greatness.

While we were away, Meg had made a discovery. After dark, she took us to a line of trees next to the runoff of a reservoir a half-mile or so from our housing tract. She showed us a sleeping bag on a mattress between two trees, hidden by some brush. She pointed to something in the bushes. "Used rubbers," she said. "Come on, let's climb." She and Devon climbed one tree and I went up another. When we were fifteen feet above the mattress, she said, "Okay, get comfortable and get ready for the show."

"What is this?" I said.

"Just wait, you'll see. Carl comes out here with his girlfriend when he gets off work. Let's just smoke and wait." She took out a pack, stuck one in her mouth and tossed the pack to me, tree to tree. I missed the pack and they plummeted down and hit the mattress.

"Shit!" she said. "Jump down there and grab those before they get here. Carl will kick the shit out of us if he finds us up here."

"What the hell is going on?"

"I told you, it's a surprise."

I was halfway down when she hissed, "Here they come. I can see them. Hurry!"

I dropped from the branches, landed wrong on my foot and twisted my ankle.

"Shit! Hurry!"

I grabbed the pack and the cigarettes that had fallen out, stuffed them in my pocket and shimmied up the tree again, my ankle aching, my heart pounding. I knew what was about to happen was going to be weird, and I'd guessed, of course, that it was going to be sex. And I was pissed at Meg for throwing the cigarettes. Carl was the meanest of her brothers, and he carried a knife. But it turned out I'd had plenty of time; it was another five minutes before Carl and his skinny girlfriend finally tumbled onto the mattress.

Carl opened a beer and lit a cigarette. They talked softly for a few minutes and began to kiss. We could see them clearly in the moonlight. He took off her clothes and I could see the patch of hair between her legs and the dark eyes of her breasts quivering up at me as Carl buried his face between her legs.

She started to writhe and moan. "Okay, okay!" she said.

Carl pulled his pants down to his knees, put on a condom, and climbed on top of her. They did it that way for a while, then she got on her knees in front of him.

She kept moaning, "Oh God, oh God," and that seemed strange to me. Was she calling out to God for forgiveness or was she thanking him?

Suddenly, Carl let out a yell and started pumping like a maniac from behind her, and then joined her in the summoning of God.

He rolled off of her and pulled his pants up. They lit cigarettes, and she thanked him and told him it was great, which seemed strange to me at the time, too, as I'd thought sex was something you essentially had to streal from girls, something you tricked them into doing with words or alcohol.

Then she told him not to fall sleep because she had to get home to babysit her sister. She got dressed and they left.

After a few quiet minutes, we climbed down from the trees.

"So, what did you think?" Meg asked.

"I thought that was some weird shit," I said.

"It was the real thing," Devon said. "The real thing."

Meg lit a cigarette and pushed the sleeping bag around with her foot. "What was so weird about it?"

"Well, the way they kept saying 'Oh God, oh God!' It was like they were holy rollers being saved."

"You're the fucking weirdo," she said. "I'm talking about what they were doing. Screwing. They were screwing. They were balling."

"Yeah, the real thing," Devon said again, shaking his head, amazed.

"I know what they were doing. I saw what they were doing. I just thought it was weird that they were both saying 'Oh God, oh God!' It sounded like they were being tortured. I know what they were doing. It's not that big a deal."

"Have you ever done it?"

"Yeah."

Devon laughed. "Liar."

I pushed him. "How would you know? I don't tell my little brother everything I do. You guys are a couple of virgins treating this like it's some big deal."

"I did it with my cousin," Meg said. "He lied to me and told me he was just gonna put his finger in because we'd been doing that since we were little."

"With your cousin?" Devon asked. "Isn't that illegal?"

"Yeah, well, nobody gave us a ticket. I didn't like it all that much. But I don't like my cousin all that much either. I beat the shit out of him the next day."

Devon picked up a box.

"Rubbers," Meg said. "Those are so the girl doesn't get

pregnant."

"You don't have to tell us everything, Meg," I said. "We know about rubbers."

Devon stepped in. "How do they work?"

She opened one and held it in her palm. She and Devon peered at it. I took a wild guess: "Unroll it." She fiddled with it and it began to unroll; she kept going until it hung there in her hand like an uninflated balloon.

"What do I do with it?" she asked.

"Well, you can't put it back, can you? Just put it in your pocket and hope he doesn't notice one is missing."

"We ruined it," she said, "so we might as well use it."

"How do you mean use it?" Devon said. "You mean really use it?"

"Hell yes! Why not? We're old enough. You're the only one here who hasn't done it. Maybe you and me should do it first."

"I don't know if I'm ready," Devon said. "Maybe you and my brother should do it first."

"Here." She handed me the rubber and started taking off her shirt.

"I'm going up the tree," Devon said.

Meg had no breasts. Though she was taller now and weighed ninety-five pounds or so, she had not grown any. Her nipples were just larger than a boy's. She unbuckled her belt, undid the buttons of her Levi's with a yank, and stepped out of them. She put her thumbs in the waistband of her tighty-whities, took them down to her knees, and paused to look at me.

"What are you waiting for?"

I took off my T-shirt. My heart was pounding, my ears ringing, and when I got my pants off the little man was pointing up. It was another entity, an entity that captured Meg's attention. "My cousin's had more skin," she said, "but yours is handsomer. How did you start when you did it?"

I put on the rubber as though I'd done it dozens of times before. "Lay down," I commanded, and I was on her almost before her back hit the sleeping bag. The compulsion had kicked in and I was drawn and driven, with no control over myself from that point forward. It felt like a kind of tender, unrelenting anger, and I knew that this deed would be done. A force stronger than anything I'd known was pulling something out of me. It crossed my mind that maybe this *was* the force of God.

"Jesus!" she said. "Hold on a second."

But I was trying to get it in, poking it around between her legs, and the sensation of it touching the soft hair and skin of her was so exquisite that I, too, called out to God—not in terror so much as in hallelujah.

"Did you piss on me?" she said as I continued to fail to make the connection.

I realized the wetness she felt was just the lubricant from the rubber and was just about to say so when I suddenly struck gold and was inside her.

We both gasped and stayed still for a moment. Then she put her arms around me to pull me close and we were, in our silence, welded. She moved under me and I responded gently back, and then we sank down into a place so dark and beautiful and bestial that we were out of time and world and all individuality. It was as if this "thing" had been waiting for us, had tricked us with the bait of her brother and his girlfriend, the rubbers, the trees, the girl having to go home to babysit. It had all been a ruse to get us into this world of strangeness where we just kept moving together for a long, long time, during which I called out to God on at least three more occasions, and Meg squealed like a kid on a rollercoaster twice.

Finally, we lay panting, as if we'd been in the longest fight of our lives. The cool of the night moved across our skin and we fell asleep.

I was dreaming of the water in the Gulf of Mexico when Devon shook me.

"We've got to get home. Mom will be pissed."

I shook Meg.

She sat up and looked around, blinking like a child. "Wow. That was the shit, wasn't it? I like it."

Meg and I stopped looking for fights and started looking for places and times to have sex. Generally, we did it outside and at night, but we would also duck into the restroom at a gas station and lock the door in the middle of the day. We went through the window at the locker room of our junior high school and did it with all the showers on, but that was pretty risky. Sometimes we'd lock her garage door from the inside and do it on a couple of sleeping bags on the cement. At night, we would use her brother's place beneath the trees, or we'd take our sleeping bags out into the desert and do it beneath the stars.

We never kissed, or said we loved each other, or promised anything except that we'd always be friends. We were not boyfriend and girlfriend. We'd found something we really liked to do, and we did it with complete abandon and ferocity. It was decades before I heard the term "fuck buddies," but, in the purest sense of the term, that's what we were. But fuck buddies implies a certain distance. One has a fuck buddy one can call when in need of sex. It's more fuck than buddy. That wasn't us. We were inseparable, and we did lots of other things besides have sex. We played baseball at the park, swam, went shooting with my father and Devon, ate watermelon, and smoked cigarettes, but we enjoyed sex more than anything else.

There were rumors around the neighborhood that Meg was a lesbian. Devon relayed them to me since nobody else would say it to my face. I asked her about this as we lay naked beneath the stars smoking cigarettes and drinking sloe gin.

"Girls? How could I do it with a girl, you friggin' idiot? They don't have dicks."

"I'm just saying, a lot of athletic girls—well, some of them—are that way. I mean—you aren't exactly girlish."

"Wouldn't want to be. I don't think about that shit. I just like to get out and do things, you know? I want to have me a nice gun, a good, fast car. I'd like to be on a goddamn baseball team, but I can't get along with the coaches or the bitches on those softball teams. I just want do cool stuff and have a few good friends."

"This is pretty cool," I said, "laying here looking at the stars, naked under the sky with plenty of smokes. Balling any time we want."

"That's right. Doesn't get any better than this."

"Nope. Screwing, smoking, drinking."

"Yep," she said. "The best."

Though we never kissed and there was no foreplay, I certainly didn't need it to get aroused. Her reaching for the buttons on her jeans was enough. I learned the more subtle aspects of lovemaking another way and from someone else.

Freshman year, I was the quarterback on the junior varsity team. I took Rena Beck to homecoming because I was expected to go, but did not mention this to Meg.

Rena was a beautiful girl—a cheerleader—with soft hair, soft skin, and soft breasts. I felt them pressed against me as we danced: globules of teenage girlhood shielded by the formal satin of her dress.

"I have to ask you," Rena said as we walked to the after-party down the street from the high school gym where we'd just been crowned king and queen. "Are you actually dating that Megan girl, or what?"

The Mojave wind was cold. I put my arm around her and kept walking. There were couples in front of us and behind us laughing and talking in the wind.

"Did you hear me?"

"No, what did you say?"

"Are you going out with that girl, Megan, the lesbian?"

"How could I date a lesbian?"

"Is she?"

"Is she what?"

"A lesbian."

"You'd have to ask her."

"I would never ask her anything. You tell me. I know you know."

"Why do you want to know?"

"I'm curious. And you're my date. I want to know if you're normal."

"She's not a dyke, trust me," I said and steered her up the walk of the party house.

Inside, there was a keg and a hundred people laughing and talking. They sounded like crows all cawing at once, the way crows do when they settle in the treetops at the end of the day.

Rena got drunk for the "first friggin' time" in her life and we found an empty bedroom. We kissed for a while, she beer-burped into my mouth, and I eventually got her panties off. She was so soft I was afraid I was hurting her—so soft, in fact, that I put my lips between her legs and began kissing her. She writhed, squirmed, and finally demanded, "Do it— now!" I took off my suit pants, put on one of Meg's brother's rubbers, and we did it.

She fell asleep afterward and I stared into the darkness, her head on my shoulder, trying to compare this with what Meg and I did. I had done something to Rena, willing as she might have been, but Meg and I did it together. "Not comparable," I said aloud, slipping into a deep quarterback sleep.

It was 3 AM by the time someone gave us a ride home. Rena rested against me like a kitten, curled with her paws beneath her chin, deep in her own thoughts. My arm was around her and I felt fraudulently heroic there in the back seat. It was as if I was playing the quarterback in a movie. I walked her up to the door and we kissed. Her eyes were hardly open. "You're normal, all right," she said. "Will you call me?"

"For what?"

She opened her eyes wide. "What a jerk." She unlocked the door and went in without a backward glance.

Meg didn't ask about homecoming and nothing changed between us. I contemplated calling Rena to explain I was hungover and groggy just like her, and, of course, I intended to call. But I didn't. Besides, what would she want me to do? Take her to the movies? Meet her family? No thanks. I much preferred Meg's company, and our sex, to the soft theft between Rena's legs, the thought of which was almost embarrassing.

Once football season was over, Meg and I went hunting a lot more. We shot pheasant and quail as their seasons came and went. We shot jackrabbits with .22 pistols and, late one night when her mother was sick in bed with a fever, we stole her car and drove two hundred miles to stay in a run-down roadside motel. We played cards, drank, had a shitload of sex, then got some coffee and headed back toward home.

We stopped to get some gas just as a couple of rednecks walked into the station with a gas can. They were in their thirties, half drunk, and fat. One paid the attendant, and the other stuck the nozzle in the can and said to Meg, "Are you a girl or a hippy?"

"Take a guess, you ignorant son of a bitch," she replied.

"I say you're a boy hippy who just got his hair cut," the other said.

Meg took two steps forward and caught him square in the forehead with a perfect overhand right.

The big corn-fed fool fell back on his ass and the gas can went flying.

The other one came at her, but I caught him in the back of the head and felt the middle finger on my right hand break.

He turned quickly and came back at me. He should have gone down with that punch, so he was obviously tougher than he looked. The four of us went at it by the pumps beneath the flickering station lights and it was a hell of a brawl.

Meg took her guy out fairly fast—Jesus, she could fight—and he was curled up by the Regular pump holding his balls.

My guy could really take a punch and he eventually caught me hard in the face a couple of times. I was on the ropes when I saw Meg behind him. As he prepared to drop me, she kicked him hard between the legs like she was punting a football. He dropped to his knees and I put everything I had left into the the hand without the broken finger and did to him was he'd been about to do to me. It was over.

"I had to call the cops," the station attendant said from the doorway of the garage. "You kids better get the hell out of here. Thanks for kicking the shit out of these two, though. Bastards always come in here and give us a hard time."

"Why'd you call the cops then?" Meg asked.

"It's the station rules. Now git."

We jumped back into her mom's car and took off with the wired-on muffler rattling and the tires squealing. We laughed and rehashed the fight, sailing down the highway at seventy without a care in the world. Somewhere near Boron, we stopped at an abandoned railroad station, broke into the building with a sleeping bag, and had sex on the floor of the women's bathroom. We'd stopped for ice and band-aids and when we'd fucked ourselves out, Meg held the ice to my face and my hand. There was a tenderness in the way she bent over me that was new. In the stillness of that moment, I saw that she truly did have the beginnings of breasts now. She lifted the ice and "kissed the boo-boo." We laughed at that and lit cigarettes, at peace. It was our last adventure.

My aunt Rose was killed in a car accident on Easter morning and my family drove nonstop to Texas for the funeral. We were there for a week and it was a sad drive back, with my mother crying and my father trying in vain to keep his eyes on the road as he comforted her. We got home after midnight and the moon was full. The four of us got out and stood in the driveway, stretching.

"It's good to be home," my mother said. It was the first sentence I'd heard her speak in a week that was not broken with a sob.

"It is," my father said, "it is."

I agreed, but as I looked across the street at Meg's house, something wasn't right. Her brother's motorcycle wasn't parked on the porch, her mom's beat-up Ford with the tail light lens taped on was also gone, and the moon seemed to be pouring into the naked windows like a searchlight. I walked across the street.

"Where's he going?" I heard my mother ask.

The house was empty. There were still things in it: a broken chair, a box of magazines, and a belt on the kitchen floor. But the red-headed people were gone, having moved out, no doubt, in the same fashion they arrived, with the rattling trucks of uncles and cousins, fleeing the innumerable financial ghosts that plagued the family: unpaid rent, huge, accumulated utility bills, and distant relatives trying to collect debts run up by Meg's vanished father. She'd told me about these things, but their oppressive reality never sank in for me. I thought she would live here forever. I opened the garage door. Inside was a mess, but her brothers' tools—probably the most valuable and well-kept possession the family owned— had disappeared from the dilapidated workbench. My father walked up behind me.

"Looks like they're gone. Did you know they were moving?"

"No. No idea."

"She does have our phone number, right?"

"I don't know. Maybe."

"Maybe they moved across town. Found cheaper rent or something."

"Yeah."

He lit a cigarette. "Poverty," he said. "I hate it."

I didn't see Meg for eleven years. I graduated, got drafted, went to Nam, returned, took LSD, played semi-pro football for all of five weeks, and generally grew into a confused wreck of a human being—but I had not forgotten her. I'd called information for every town and city in California, but couldn't track the family down. More than likely they'd used a relative's name to get phone service, as they owed lots of money to various phone companies. Meg was not allowed to use the phone and I'd never seen her even use a pay phone. "Poverty," I'd say after each attempt. "I hate it."

I was driving through Boron one Sunday in the spring of 1973, on my way to see my parents. I stopped in a mini-mart to gas up and was standing in line at the cash register with a candy bar and a Coke. The woman ahead of me had three small kids tugging on her dress and slugging each other.

She smacked one of them on the arm. "Knock it off—now!" she told him.

Her hair was shoulder-length, reddish and unwashed. Her shoulders were bony beneath the thin material of the dress. When she took her change, there was something in the way she moved that told me without a doubt it was Meg.

She turned and took a step toward the door, but glanced over her shoulder, saw me, and stopped cold. One of the kids ran into the back of her legs.

"Is that you?" she said.

"Yes," I said. "It's me."

"Goddamn! It is you."

"It is. It's me."

It was her, but she could have passed for her mother: the same haggard look, the empty eyes, the deepening lines around her mouth as if she hadn't had a drink of water in a year. It was Meg, but she was a woman now, not the cocky boyish girl I'd known.

"You never called, Meg," I said, and laughed.

"I lost your number."

A hulking man stepped inside the mart. He was unshaven and sweating, and could have passed for one of the guys we'd fought in the gas station the night we stole her mother's car.

"Shit, honey, I been sittin' in the goddamn truck for half an hour."

"I'm coming," she said. She smiled at me and her eyes shone with everything we'd ever done and all the longing we'd felt for the adventures we thought were to come. But there was softness in her eyes now, a fondness—perhaps it was having children. And there was, too, all the weariness, sadness, and crushed ambition of the destiny that was hers, her mother's, and her children's.

My skin tingled and my eyes welled. We were silent, but something deep and open pulsed between us for a few moments before she followed her hick and her children out to the truck and home to whatever ramshackle house they rented, with a dead motorcycle parked on the porch.

I paid for the gas and the Coke and candy, and by the time I stepped out of the store, back into the dry summer heat, she was long gone.

I stood there for a few moments, staring up into the hard blue sky. Then I got into my car, leaned my head against the steering wheel, and cried.

EVERYTHING EXISTS

July 31

The trail we follow leads to the mountains. The air down here on the plain is dry and windless. After six days of walking, we have stopped for a two-day rest.

Yesterday I asked our guide, Shejon Bolod, about the thick scars on his back. He laughed, saying he's told so many tall tales about those scars, he's forgotten how he actually got them. He didn't volunteer to tell me any of the tall tales, but I'm not offended. I like his attitude better than that of people back home who are always willing to drone on about their emotional scars—victims, as they are, of bad childhoods, bad marriages, or the economy—utterly predictable laments. I remove myself quickly from their company, leaving a sarcastic remark in my wake, if possible, to give notice of my indifference. Everyone suffers. Get over it.

This evening's spicy dinner was conjured from roots and spices by the crew's two women, one of whom has wondrous breasts. The men reverently watch her languorous waltz from task to task, the half-fluid lobes following in sway a moment behind any change of direction, their perfect ripeness always on the verge of overflowing their flawless form. An object of adoration and mystery, she hums as she works. Her large hands grip the hilt of her knife with a slack and casual confidence born of repetition. Someone would have made a play for this cook, I'm sure, but for her extreme height. She must be near seven feet, and her eyes, as if in response to the altitude, bulge ominously from their too-small sockets.

August 2
Each day walking across the plain is a lifetime whose end is a well-earned sleep as deep as death. The gargantuan emptiness of the plain leaves more space for dreams; they seem to take place in the air. Two nights ago I dreamed my wife was here. We made love slowly in the sweetness of the dirt, only to be discovered by the seven-foot cook and her wild alarming eyes. I awoke, and now I walk again.

August 6
So little time to write as we grind out the days toward the mountains. We are up before the sun. The Dragno men mumble their morning liturgy with heavy-lidded eyes, and the women brew the cocaine-strength, dirt-like tea that keeps them joking and laughing beneath their heavy loads until we stop mid-morning for our breakfast of grain cakes and water.

By noon, we are deep into the walk. When we begin to tire in the afternoon, the Dragnos get out their walking drums. They play several in echoing unison up and down the line. A light drum of lambskin and reinforced balsa, it is easily played on the move in a deep, exotic marching rhythm. The walking drum takes over one's limbs and makes the body lighter. For the last few hours, we march silently to the ghostly call of the drums.

At long last, Shejon Bolod silences the drums with a shout. A sigh of relief travels up and down the line as we stop.

We rest for an hour, and then the other men and I set up camp while the women prepare the meal. Everything we eat is either root, dried fruit, or grain, so I've become an involuntary vegetarian. But no two meals taste the same; the women are wizards of spice and texture. Though I long for the substantial feel of meat between my teeth and the drowsy wellbeing of carnivorous digestion, I am trimmer and my skin glows, clinging to my features with a new and ruddy firmness. Despite my red hair and pale complexion, I am becoming, like the Dragnos, a human gazelle, streamlined for traveling distances.

August 7
Another dream of home last night, sitting beneath the awning on the porch of the new house. It was pouring and I listened to the drum and trickle of the raindrops on the roof. I stood and went inside.

There, on the hardwood floor, my wife was calmly copulating with another man. Seeing me, she jumped off him and shoved him out the side door. "I thought you were still walking toward the mountains," she said, as if that were a perfectly reasonable explanation.

I woke with tears blurring the stars. Their twinkling, I'm told, travels four hundred years to reach the prism of our gaze. Tomorrow, I will forget my self-pity and walk again.

August 8
During the day we are strangers walking together, but in the evening we stare into the crackling fire and talk about life. The Dragnos talk in their language, even as we speak English. From their tone, the Dragnos, too, are speaking about life: how it unfolds, the dangers, the sweetness, and the brevity. The farther you are from civilization, the more you talk about life itself, and not petty things happening in the world. The high air of the plain does this to us.

August 15
After a thunderstorm drew near then dissipated, an elderly Dragno walking ahead of me dropped dead in his tracks. He didn't call out or clutch his chest. He simply crumbled mid-step like a collapsing building. The fingers on his left hand twitched a few times, and then he was still.

Shejon Bolod explained that Death had ridden the thunderstorm to find the old man. His body was as limp as clothing dropped next to the bed before sleep. I lost my fear of death for a moment. We stopped for the day. They said prayers and burned his body. It sounded like a choir from Purgatory and smelled like barbecue.

We are approaching a mountain. What appeared a sheer, monolithic protrusion into the sky is actually becoming the earth beneath our feet. It rises with an immense grace and gradual incline that will soon give way to excruciating steepness. All the walking has been worth it. Now, sleep.

August 26
Nothing to write today. Just walking.

September 14
I am determined to keep this journal on a more regular basis. We are in our second week of ascent and I have not documented a single impression of this slow and astounding climb. It is dangerous, but the patient Dragnos know the trail and keep us at a crawl.

Even birds are less active at this altitude. The tough foliage seems to grow out of the rock, and the occasional mountain goat stares at us from a distance as if we are insane. But I do love this—I am most alive approaching mysterious destinations. I just heard a bird cry out in the dark. Exotic and moving. Must sleep.

September 20

Our first contact with the Borsogan mountain people came this morning. They are naked and tall with narrow faces, full lips, and shaggy hair. Never have I seen such calmness in human beings as in the party of men who came out to meet us.

They walked up at midday when we were resting and sat down without any greeting. They spoke with a Dragno who spoke their dialect. The Westerners among us stared, but they were unperturbed and only glanced at us in the way one looks at strangers at a cocktail party. They have the physiques of gazelles and beautiful strong teeth, huge light brown eyes, irises flecked with gray and green. Their body language is unreadable. It is difficult to tell young from old, though the ones talking seemed to be younger.

One fellow fondled himself to erection as he absent-mindedly stared off into the clouds. Another went to sleep.

Suddenly, as if roused by an undetectable cue, they got up and ambled off. All the English speakers pounced on the interpreter, who simply said they'd welcomed us to stay a few days in their village. They'd spoken of recent good fishing caused by the birth of many babies in the village.

September 22

We reached the crest of the mountain, walked for a day across a wind-swept plateau, and now we descend. My guess is a volcano formed the valley below us. The soil is obviously rich, since everything down there is green. The valley looks to be five or six miles across and maybe two miles wide. In the middle there is a large lake bluer than the sky. How is it fed? Certainly there are no underground springs up here. By rain?

Our descent will take two days. When we stop we'll have to sleep on little shelves of solid earth jutting out from the steep decline, a party of thirty or so perched on the bleak side of the valley wall looking down into a peaceful dale from which no sound rises.

September 24
Yesterday we reached the valley floor. The smells are wonderful. You would think there would be more trees, but all the green we saw from above was tall grasses. The soil is absolutely black. Snakes are everywhere and plenty of wild goats. Few birds, though.

Tomorrow we will reach the village by the lake. We have seen a few more Borsogan mountain people. They don't appear curious about us, yet I am told they don't see many outsiders. I have not seen a stitch of clothing, though we have yet to see any women.

September 25
We arrived in the Borsogan village today. It was good to see people living real lives. My fellow travelers and I are, by comparison, spores traveling the wind. But these people aren't going anywhere. They are simply with each other in the place they live. They talk and laugh. They call out from time to time to the children who play carelessly as puppies.

But let me begin again. At midday we heard dogs barking in the distance. Another hour of walking and we caught sight of the village. Soon we were close enough to see people moving.

We entered the village as quietly as monks, with our heads bowed. The children ran to greet us. These beautiful little beings danced around us naked and dirty from play. They poked at us with small fingers, smiling and chirping at each other in the soft sounds of their language. I picked up one of the little girls and said hello to her in English. She smiled directly into my eyes for a moment, then giggled hysterically as I put her down.

The adults came to greet us as naked as their children, but walking slowly. They smiled and gazed at us with mild curiosity. The children operate with complete abandon, while everything the adults do is slow and deliberate.

There are some unoccupied huts on the far side of the village that the Borsogan have prepared for us. These huts are made of grass bundled tightly and woven together. The roofs are thick and slick with some sort of waterproofing. The interpreter explained that the Borsogan would bring us fish and vegetables when the sun went down. With these arrangements completed, we were paraded through the village with the flock of laughing children running behind us.

The women are thin and small-breasted, not a one that would be considered ample in the Western world. Perhaps it is the lack of body fat that makes them so. Even those who sit in front of their huts nursing babies have puny, wide-set mammary bulbs. Tufts sprout from their armpits and their legs are slightly fuzzy. From between their legs leap dense bushes. Perhaps, going naked generation after generation, they have evolved thicker protection for their nether regions. If I was imagining some romantic encounter here, that fantasy has been put to rest. I'd sooner make love to the tall cook with the bulging eyes.

I have a hut with a Dragno and another American, a boring guy who spent some time in prison for embezzling. We will be comfortable here. My grass bed is heavenly. Now for a nap.

September 28
The Borsogan come alive at night. Everything important besides fishing and the care of infants is done after the sun goes down. The children own the day and go to sleep early, exhausted from play. For the adults, socializing is nocturnal. They wait like cats for the golden disc of the sun to disappear behind the rim of the mountains. The darker it gets, the more animated they become. While it is a relief not to walk every day, I'm restless for some kind of activity, and tonight we are invited to a wedding.

It was a wedding unlike any I've ever seen. The Nomtissa came down to officiate. His title means "Old Man" according to the translator. There is only one Nomtissa at a time and he must live alone. He can be visited and consulted, but he cannot live in the village. And his title was certainly fitting— his wrinkles had wrinkles, as they say.

Do they say that? I have been gone so long from home that common figures of speech seem not to make sense. I doubt the evidence of my past existence. For all I know, my memories are dreams from which I am awaking. There is nothing here to orient me.

The ceremony took place down by the lake. The Nomtissa walked around and around the couple, mumbling and whining and occasionally giving the young groom a solid smack with his leathery old palm. There was a best man of sorts, but she was a woman who looked to be in her late fifties. She followed the Nomtissa around, pleading with him as he grumbled and slapped the groom.

The wedding party consisted of the entire village and they watched these proceedings with rapt attention. Apparently the wedding is a kind of test, and if the Nomtissa does not approve, the couple's relationship may end there on the spot. This, we are told, does happen from time to time and a "Dead Wedding" is a source of social agony for the family. So everyone was very alert. All eyes were on the Nomtissa.

After an hour of this drudgery beneath a moon, so full the disc of its reflection was huge upon the lake, the older woman seemed finally to have convinced the Nomtissa. With a final groan of resignation, he let her lead him away and a rousing cheer went up. Everyone rushed to embrace and kiss the newlyweds. Some of the men even smacked him the way the Nomtissa had.

The older woman led the Nomtissa to the edge of the

village. There she stopped and he went on alone.

Then the celebration started. It wasn't that we travelers were ignored so much as we just didn't know what to do. There was food, dancing, and absurdly loud conversation. I was content to sit and watch. Usually I love to dance, but their rhythmless dancing to the inconsistent beat of the drumming was something I'd never attempt to mimic.

The young women were in small groups and carefully chaperoned by adults of both sexes. Older women monitored the young men individually; their manners were somehow tutorial, as if they were mentors. They were stern and a little intimidating with their lined faces and saggy breasts. Women of this age appear to have great power here. But if the menopausal coaches have husbands themselves, they must have been with the groups of older men moving about like teenaged boys at a carnival. The children were complete hellions by Western standards. As the celebration wore on, they dropped, exhausted and filthy, wherever they happened to be and fell to sleep.

As the celebration continued, the adult dancing grew suggestive. Some adult men grasped their erections and danced in circles. Women stroked their husbands or held their testicles. Men cupped pudendas reverently or massaged spousal buttocks. Yet the party was certainly no orgy. The respectful dancing and fondling appeared quite relaxed, with monogamous boundaries unchallenged—no one seemed overly aroused, nor was there anything aggressive about any of it. Weird.

My own weddings were not so innocent. After the first, my attorney would attend, taking mental notes, I'm sure, for the time when the flowers, high hopes and champagne gave way to blood, thorns and law. Only my current wife interrupts that stream of disappointments. And how do I repay her? By attending weddings on mountaintops and watching people fondle each other.

My wife and I will both sleep alone tonight in separate worlds. And so I scratch out these few words no one will ever read while the embezzler snores but yards away. Stranger than dreams, these adventures.

September 30
Woke up this morning optimistic but feverish. Something I ate. Knots in the gut. But I walked around the village feeling quite at home, though we've been here only a few days. Returned to the hut quickly, however. Hope I feel better tomorrow.

September 31
Couldn't sleep last night. Fever. Horrendous dreams. Tired.

November 3
If I have to be this sick, let me die.

November 29
Not sure if it really is November 29th. After what I believe was three days, I started scratching marks in the dirt next to my mat to keep track. Though I was delirious, I felt compelled to keep track of the date, but when I finally woke, I had to rely on an estimate of the days from the translator.

I don't want to slip into timelessness and be carried to my death unaware of my birthday or Christmas. These small temporal islands in eternity seem important when you are far from home and dying. When the members of the walking party came in to say goodbye, I thought I had died. I wanted to shout out that I was alive, but I couldn't open my eyes or mouth. The leader whispered in my ear that they had to leave before the rains came. The expedition was already a week behind from our windy delays on the plateau. Someone would return after the rains.

When my head finally cleared, the translator they left

behind for me explained my situation. I wanted to shoot the scrawny bastard. But now that I am well, I am grateful that they left a translator and I understand the party's decision. I would have done the same.

The illness took me deeper into the world of dreams and beyond the world created by everyday assumptions. My dreams were ceaseless and without context or past—leaping full-blown and vivid into my mind, one after another.

Now I am awake in this dream, stuck here with these people, in this hut, in this grassy landscape. Tomorrow, I will walk down to the lake and bathe. I am filthy.

November 30
Didn't bother to put on clothes. I just walked down to the lake as naked as the rest of the village to wash the dried sweat and stink from my body in the cool lake. No one gave me a second glance. Perhaps they'd all come through the hut to view me in my delirium.

Women bathed themselves and their children. I guess they do wash the youngsters occasionally. We could see the fishing boats in the distance. The water was cold, pure and clear.

But I must rest. Even this short bathing expedition exhausted me. The strange sickness I had will be forever undiagnosed. But of what use is a label for the malady here, on a mountain with no doctors or hospitals? Let's just say, for some reason I was sick. That will have to do. Boccho, the translator, did tell me that the Nomtissa was summoned to look at me. He'd closed his eyes and communed with some entity or another. On his way out, he announced that I would not die. He was right and sent no bill, so I'm happy.

December 2
All this grass but no trees. Why no trees? It rained for most of the day. The clouds pour in over the rim of the valley and

dump their water into the basin as if preparing a bath for the gods. The surface of the lake is a trillion dancing dimples for hours. When it has ended, the still-green valley is heavenly: silent, immaculate, cool. The lake is again an expanse of azure glass.

I feel stronger. Tonight, I'll go out walking and learn a little more about the people with whom I'll be spending the next year.

December 3
The grass roofs are absolutely waterproof. Fortunately, the rain slowed a bit, but now we are engulfed in fog. I learned a lot last night. Boccho and I talked to an old woman sitting under the porch of her hut. People sit under these porches when it rains—nothing more than a grass roof and four posts made of bound and twisted reeds. They squat, talk, and watch the rain.

When I asked about their marriage customs, she explained that girls are married around age thirteen, soon after their first period, to men aged eighteen to twenty. She must be a virgin when she marries.

Men are another matter. When a boy reaches puberty, he is apprenticed to a post-menopausal woman. I apply Western terminology here since the old woman's descriptions of the various stages of human sexual development were circumspect and poetic. What we would call puberty for boys, she called "the age of spitting." It took me a while to figure out that she meant semen and not saliva.

Maturity for the girl was described as "coming into the Sun." Menopause, of course, was "leaving the Sun." Somehow this is all tied into the Sun providing fish when there are babies born. I'll ask about that later. Once the terminology was clear, I was amazed at the complexity and practicality of their social structure. I'll put it down here, as I understand it now, in hope that I'll come to understand the nuances later.

This apprenticeship of boys to older women is sexual in nature. The old women sleep with the boys and teach them about sex and marriage. This is made possible by the fact that marriage ends here when a woman is no longer fertile. "When she moves out of the Sun, she is done." Her husband must leave the home and live alone or with other old men. These old men who are exiled from their wives were, themselves, as boys, taken from their mothers and fathers and given into the tutorial custody of the old women. A boy is considered a man when he reaches this age of ejaculation and is given the mentor his parents have selected. She is his "mornicsum." I have employed a phonetic spelling here. The mornicsum's job is highly respected. A woman who does it well is in demand. If the boy she mentors pleases his wife, becoming a good husband and a respected person in the community, she will have her pick of young boys. A bad marriage may also be attributed to her. If the boy is a lout, she is scorned and will live alone. No doubt there are plenty of politics involved in the placing of these boys. The best mornicsums are probably talent scouts and diplomats.

The belief is that mentoring young men extends the life of a mornicsum and renders them content and wise. Who could argue that? It is also believed that her characteristics will show up in the children of the boys she ushered into manhood. Interesting genetic theory.

While the boy lives with his mornicsum, she teaches him all she knows about married life. Her most important job is to train him erotically. This makes perfect sense—the raging urges of a teenage boy go to good use in satisfying and keeping vital an aging woman who cannot become pregnant. His initiation into adulthood is a second eroticized childhood. Freud would love this.

After a couple of years, he is ready for marriage. His mornicsum, who will have been scouting the crop of pubescent girls, selects his wife. When the bride-to-be comes into the

Sun, the mentor goes to her home and examines her vagina and menstrual blood. This is done at noon when the sun is directly overhead in the sky. People gather around and watch. Satisfied that the girl is ready and the plumbing acceptable, the mornicsum will make her decision. The engagement is brief, as the marriage must be celebrated as soon as she stops bleeding. The Nomtissa oversees this, and he must approve of the match.

The old woman explained that mentors come under criticism if they take too much time finding a suitable bride. Selfish mentors grow attached to the boys and want to keep them for themselves. But a check and balance system is in place. Such a woman will have a hard time getting another boy, and families have been known to come and retrieve their sons if a mentorship stretches beyond a decent period. Such cases can also be taken before the Nomtissa.

The Nomtissa is the final word on everything. He lives up the hillside. I see people headed there with fish and other supplies. An ancient woman always leads the way.

December 5
Last night I saw the strangest girl. She was gray! I am talking Confederate army gray. She must be an albino and this gray the result of the stray albino gene mixed with the color of her people. She looked to be in her early twenties, but it was hard to tell. My albino theory was confirmed when I got close enough to see that the irises of her eyes were cherry red. Anatomically she was normal—narrow face and small breasts, wide deep chest for breathing the thin air. And her hair was blond. She stood out like a lighthouse among the black-haired villagers. I watched her grinding meal with a few other girls. These people don't mind if you stare. Here one has the freedom to look or ignore. There is no embarrassment, like the mountain man who met us on the trail who sat fondling himself while the other men talked to us. The women are

just as bad—they scratch and tug at that huge bush between their legs as if trying to rout some small animal that has taken refuge there. Then they return to preparing food with those same fingers.

For this and other reasons, I confess I am homesick for civilization. I long to sit fully clothed with my wife in a café and order coffee before a meal. I want to read the paper and talk with her about household and political things. And in that café, I will occasionally imagine what the waitress or the woman seated by the door might look like without her clothes. The waitress would not dig her fingernails into her pubic hair for a brisk scratch before she handed me my pancakes. And when I went home I would have the pleasure of taking my wife's clothes off before we made love. Stripping away layer after layer of civilization until I beheld the protected flower of her nudity unexposed to the elements and the jaded eyes of others. I yearn for privacy and I miss my wife terribly, knowing that I will not see her for at least another year. When I am more than six months late she begins to worry—and to get angry. Someday I might return to find her gone.

December 6
Another wedding soon. I witnessed the selection of the bride today. Walking back from the lake, I came upon a crowd around one particular hut. An old woman stood in the doorway talking to the father of the potential bride. The mornicsum spoke in gruff, accusing tones. She waved her hands and spat on the ground. The father hung his head, never looking her in the eye.

Finally, he turned and said something to the people inside and a young girl appeared. He pushed her gently out into the crowd and they stepped back to make a clearing for her. Her head hung and she rubbed her eyes. The mornicsum, followed by her embarrassed mentee, walked around the poor girl making guttural noises, spitting and shaking her head in disapproval.

At this point, the mentee said something and the old woman slapped him. He fell silent and his mornicsum gestured for him to look the other way. She ordered the girl to sit down and spread her legs. Right there in front of everyone she examined the girl's vagina. The girl was calm, looking up at the woman as if seeking her approval. I looked away to observe the intense expressions on the faces of the crowd, and when I looked back, the old woman was holding a bloody finger up to the sun. She made a pronouncement and a murmur of approval spread through the crowd. The smiling future bride got up and went back in the hut. The father stepped up to the old woman, perhaps to offer his thanks, but she pivoted and strode away, followed by the puppy-dog groom. Members of the crowd congratulated the father. This evening we heard that the wedding is on. The excitement in the village is palpable.

December 7
Now that I'm healthy, I have lots of energy but not much to do. I had been accustomed to walking all day across the plain, so now I feel trapped. I asked through the interpreter, Boccho, if I could go fishing with the men. They said that would be bad for fishing. The Sun would not recognize me. She would be confused and withhold fish. She? I was disappointed by this prohibition, but interested in the Sun as a woman.

I had Boccho ask how they know the Sun is a she, and how do they know what confuses her? The answer came back quickly. The Sun has always been a she and if she wants us to know something, she will tell the Nomtissa. No arguing with an answer like that.

In fact, there's no arguing with anyone here. People don't really talk that much. Most verbal are the post-menopausal women—"achvas," they are called. They do a great deal of expostulating compared to the younger population, walking around in the evening commenting on everything. If they have a mentee, he is in tow and listening intently. A proud and haughty bunch of old birds.

December 8
I have been summoned to see the Nomtissa. This is big deal, and today I was the object of some enigmatic looks. Usually, one woman brings my food. Today, there were four and they stayed to watch me eat. I am a monkey in a cage.

For all I know, the Nomtissa has decided to have me executed. I couldn't offer up much of a defense. So this may be the last entry in my journal. I doubt anyone will ever read these words anyway. But if you are reading them, at whatever moment in the infinite stillness of time, let me say this: I am not afraid of death. It can only be a vast and virgin adventure. I have seen infants born and I saw the old Dragno die on the plain. They were both horrific and beautiful moments, and death will come when it will come. Let the Nomtissa sentence me to the ultimate adventure. I can only pray he has a painless plan of execution.

December 9
Let me begin slowly, one detail at a time. The Nomtissa was beyond anything I could have expected. A little after dark, a convocation of four achvas and a man came to my hut. Boccho and I followed them up the hill to the Nomtissa's hut. The procession was quiet and ceremonious. The women looked down at their feet and muttered what sounded like a droning prayer under their breath. I looked at the sky. The clear evening twilight hung vast and transient above us. The stillness of the earth was unbearably beautiful. What better time to die?

The Nomtissa greeted me with a broad toothless smile. He motioned for me to sit. To my astonishment, the oldest achva present went directly to the promontory of woven mats where he sat and took his wrinkled member between her lips. He nodded approvingly, but motioned her away after he looked into my eyes. His eyes were dark and keen, and I could see this was a man of curiosity. His smile put me at ease. Another old woman served a beverage from a clay pot, and we passed a dipper around the room. The drink was cool and tasted of mint and roots.

The Nomtissa exchanged a few words with the achva whose fellatio he'd rejected, then addressed Boccho. As he did so, he watched my face and nodded slowly as Boccho turned to me and explained in English: "He says that you are welcome here. He was sorry to hear you were sick. He believes there were chips of moon stuck in the side of the mountain when you came up. When you were sleeping, one of these must have found its way into your mouth. He says you should always sleep with your mouth closed when climbing mountains. The closer to the Sun you get, the more likely you are to be attacked by these stray chips. He says the chips are good for plants but not for people.

"He says you staying here has caused some confusion. He has tried to explain your situation to the Sun, but has not had much luck. Sometimes the Sun is not good at understanding human matters. After all, she has the whole sky and earth to take care of and grows impatient with long explanations.

"But what concerns the Nomtissa is this. You are here. You are a man. You have no wife. Therefore, you are holding back your own spitting from the Sun. The Sun is confused and this might affect the number of fish she puts in the lake. We must understand her position. She is responsible for making life. If she is upset or confused, fish and rain might be withheld while she tries to figure things out. If there are people who are not trying to make children for the Sun, life will become lopsided and the women will go crazy. Once the women begin to go crazy, it takes years to bring things back into balance. Men, on the other hand, are always crazy, so it does not affect them."

Boccho stopped and again the Nomtissa talked for several minutes. Boccho's usual cavalier manner vanished; he was in a state of deep concentration. This I attributed to the Nomtissa's strong presence. There is a purity of intent about him. Watching him speak, I could not imagine him being dishonest. He impressed me as being sensitive in an almost Western fashion, unlike the mountain people as a whole, who seem oblivious to the feelings of those around them— especially mine. But the Nomtissa was earnest and obviously concerned about me, as well as his own people.

"The Nomtissa would like you to become married," Boccho resumed. "In fact, your presence here has brought him hope in regards to another problem he has been negotiating with the Sun for a long time. There is a girl in the village he thinks was conceived of the Moon rather than the Sun. Her mother was sleeping with her legs open and a chip of the Moon entered her. The Sun mistook this for the spit of a man and grew the chip into a baby. But she came out wrong. She is a good girl, but no mornicsum will allow her boy to marry her. They are afraid things would go wrong. You would be the perfect mate because you, too, are a strange color. If you marry this girl, the Sun will be at ease. Fishing will be good and the rain will continue to come. The Nomtissa says he believes you are a dream of the Sun; she made you while she was asleep and burned you. That could be why your hair is red. This is his theory. But however you were made, the Nomtissa wants you to do as he suggests so that things will go well for everyone."

Boccho finished. Silence. I felt everyone's eyes upon me. I wanted to say I was already married and that I did not believe in the Sun, and that while the Moon chip theory was interesting, I hardly felt it explained my illness or the albino girl. Instead I said, "Tell the Nomtissa I will do whatever he thinks is best. Thank him and his people for their warm hospitality." The interpreter spoke and the Nomtissa smiled. He honored me again with the warm approval of his gaze, then turned to the women and barked instructions in gruff, short phrases. Their heads bent in supplication and the oldest achva crawled forward to offer him more oral service, but he slapped the top of her head and pointed her back to her place.

"He's giving them hell for misjudging you," Boccho explained. "He accuses them of being arrogant and narrow-minded. He says the Sun will not be pleased to know the reports they have given him about you were wrong. They told him you were a pile of Moon shit."

The Nomtissa returned his attention to me. His look was long. I held his gaze, then bowed my head slightly. He turned to the oldest achva and barked a single command. Boccho snickered but didn't tell me until we were walking down the path to the village what was so funny. "That old woman, Choheh, is going to be your mentor," he giggled. I stopped in my tracks. He continued. "The Nomtissa said everything has to be done right. You've got to live with her for a month before you can marry the gray girl. He's shortening the usual two-year period."

I looked back at the hut, wondering if I could petition for a stay of execution. "Don't even try," Boccho said. "You got off easy. I thought they were going to drown you. It's only a month. He could have made it four years."

So that is my situation. I thought I was going to die, but instead I am beginning a new life with a new wife, if I can only survive the mentorship.

December 10
This morning, a small convocation of Borsogan were waiting when I stepped from my hut. They had come to deliver me to Choheh, my newly appointed mornicsum. And so they did, walking at a ceremonial pace, as if on a funeral march.

She was waiting, a steaming cup of root drink in one hand and a broom made of a stick and twigs in the other. She dismissed the party with an impatient flick of her broom and ushered me inside. My satchel safely stashed in a corner of the hut, she motioned for me to sit on a mat near the door. I then watched as she swept every square inch of the packed dirt floor with stooped and fanatic thoroughness. Her face is much like the floor: worn, smooth, and clean. She is thin as a rail, with deflated breasts and root-like hands. Her eyes are keen and quick, and her smile reveals teeth worn to nubs. But her hair, though streaked with gray, is thick and vibrant. I have the unnerving feeling that she could beat me in a fistfight.

I fell asleep late in the afternoon watching her clean fish and woke to the smell of that fish cooking on the fire in the center of the hut. She chuckled to see me eat, for some reason, and I chuckled to see her chuckle. This was our first real interaction.

Afterward, she brought out a small gourd of smelly fish oil. She coated her hands with it and, scooting close to me, massaged my feet with great concentration. It was uncomfortable at first, but twenty minutes later, I was euphoric. Her hands are a marvel: strong, gentle, and unobtrusively intimate. By the time she finished, my feet were dreaming and I could hardly open my eyes.

The Moon was rising when we went out to socialize. His ambient light washed everything in pale visibility. Choheh paraded me around with impudence. People nodded, looked me over, and then offered us root drink. I tagged along like a walking trophy for this old bird, leaning against a post while she squatted with some other old women to gossip, laugh, and hiss. She is much the mother superior, Choheh. Of course, she wasn't quite so regal a few nights ago, scurrying across the floor to suck the Nomtissa's dong, but I suppose every society must have its class structure. Tonight she was reigning queen, chosen by the Nomtissa to do the bidding of the Sun for the good of the village.

She sleeps across from me now, a naked shadow, quiet as death. My pen scratches across the paper and I long for home, for America, for hamburgers, movies, newspapers, television, cars, baseball games, lemonade, and the warm embrace of my wife between clean sheets.

December 11
Last night, I dreamed of home—my wife playing the piano, my sister whispering admonitions in my ear: "You are so talented. Don't you want a career? How were my deviled eggs?" My narcissistic nephew was there, frightening the other children, wagging a beef tongue in their faces.

So familiar, so comfortable. . . and so temporary. My visit home was disrupted by the sound of laughter and murmuring voices from outside the hut. I parted the waxed grass of the wall and peered out into the night. They were perhaps ten yards away, a couple standing, entwined in copulation beneath the Moon. He was short and stooped, she straight and slender: a squat, gnarled mass wrapped around a willowy bough, climbing her like ivy, his face pressed between her breasts. Her back arched, her face glowing in the moonlight, as she balanced on one long leg (the other drooping lifelessly over his shoulder) as he toiled away, whispering feverishly into her breasts. She giggled in waves with the rhythm of his efforts.

I felt breath on my back. The old woman was looking over my shoulder. Embarrassed by my voyeurism, I turned to slink back to my mat, but she pointed me back toward the couple. We watched, breathing quietly behind our grass veil, until they finished and parted as casually as two friends who'd met by chance and exchanged a few brief words. I feared, however, that the old woman recognized them and would expose their tryst to the informal court of the monogamous community. But if that was her intention, she did not reveal it. Besides, she had more immediate work: me.

She urged me gently to my mat and got out her oil again. This time she began with my calves and, as she traveled up my legs, I grew so light-headed I offered no resistance when she casually placed me in her mouth as she continued to massage my thighs. No matter how she repelled me in the light of day, here in the shadows, her mouth created a welcome from my body I didn't anticipate.

Never have I been so expertly treated. Her osculation was delicate as a flower and firm as a handshake. My pollen released, I floated through the remainder of my massage like a cloud gently blown toward the sea. As I hovered near the feathered edge of sleep, she brought me back again for a second coming, then a third. This was better than my dream of home. Without a word, I fear, my mentor has converted me to belief in the Sun and the Moon.

December 25
Christmas broke like any other day here on the mountain. No squealing of nieces and nephews bounding down the stairs of my sister's house to dance in anticipation before the altar of the twinkling tree. No smell of coffee and waffles as my wife and I stumble, jet-lagged and grumbling, from the guest room. No Christmas music here in the hut, just the soft crackle of the small fire and the scratch and scrape of Choheh stirring beets and broth with a crooked spoon, her deflated leathery breasts hanging flat against her mahogany trunk.

What would I get her for Christmas, given the chance? Jade earrings? Potholders? No, a state-of-the-art broom with stiff uniform bristles and a perfectly straight handle. I doubt she would use it. She smiles. The beets are done.

December 30
My time with Choheh draws to a pleasant close. Boccho

visited today to help us with the details. Through him, Choheh described her role in the village. She is second in command, answering only to the Nomtissa. She bragged about her mentees and what good husbands they are. She spoke of her own children and complained that they avoid her. She is too strong for them, apparently. She regrets that her own son had a mornicsum who was "a dead fish head with rotten teeth." As a result, he has had a bad marriage, yet he cannot come to his own mother for advice. She shook her head sadly as she relayed this to us.

She explained that she had been nervous about being my mornicsum at first, especially since she had only a month with me. But she was proud of my progress and understood now why the Nomtissa had made the mentorship so short. She guessed that I had already had a mentor at some point in the past.

She had been a little concerned about my penis. She thought because it was pale that it might have no flavor, but, she was happy to report, it tasted fine. When she asked what was wrong with the end of it, I explained that people in the village where I lived before believed fish were provided by a man who lived in a land beyond the sky and demanded the foreskins of male babies in exchange for good fishing. She laughed until she cried.

"So what does he do?" she asked through Boccho, "turn those little bits of skin into fish and drop them into the water?"

December 31
The ball in Times Square will drop without me this year. I remember one New Year's Eve my first wife and I spent together in New York. What was her name? The snow fell so deliberately as we waited for the ball to drop. I can smell, at this moment, the warmth of her scalp, but have lost her name.

No trace of snow here, just the cool of morning and the promise of a warm day beneath the benevolent Sun. Choheh sweeps the hard dirt floor as she does each morning. Last night we sat by the lake watching two full moons—one in the empty sky and one reflected on the lake's still glass.

I've grown so used to being naked now. There was a time when my nude buttocks pressed into the packed sand of the shore and the air on my testicles would have unnerved me. Last night, however, I was aroused by it. Noticing this, Choheh laid me back on the black sand, straddled me, pressed her warm womanhood onto my lips, and, reaching back, with slow milking movements, she helped me shoot my seed at the huge blank eye of the staring Moon.

January 3
My marriage is arranged. Choheh took me by the arm at noon to the hut of my betrothed, marching with proud resolve. A small crowd awaited us. She gave a shout and the girl's father came out wearing a mask. Boccho explained that he did so to hide his identity from the Sun, as superstition surrounds the gray girl. Choheh verbally abused the masked father quite theatrically and gave him a few healthy slaps before ordering him to bring out his daughter. She scowled at the frightened girl and ordered her to sit down. She probed her and held her bloody finger up for the Sun to see. She nodded her approval to the father, and we were off.

January 10
This time tomorrow, I will be married. In no way does this resemble my previous marriages. No fitting of the tux, no awkward dinners with the parents of the bride, no battle over the guest list, no bachelor party. For the first time, I will approach the altar of matrimony without a hangover. And, of course, there will be no altar at all.

I have yet to exchange a word with my bride-to-be. Our

eyes have never met. The closest I've been to her was during Choheh's anatomical examination. We share no love. But is love the basis of a good marriage? It has not been for me. The euphoria is followed by an endless expanding boredom. So what have I to lose? I go forth, a cultural bigamist with an open mind and an ambivalent heart.

January 12
A simple marriage performed by the Nomtissa, a procession leading us to our hut, and now, after the wedding celebration: shock and exhaustion. I expected a shy bride whom I would initiate into the subtleties of conjugal bliss, per my mornicsum's instructions. Instead, I was cast, phallus first, into the embrace of a lioness. Virgin or no, she is voracious.

January 14
My new wife seems content. She is cleaning the hut before we go out to socialize. Our communication is obviously limited. I speak little of her language and she speaks none of mine. As with Choheh, there is much pointing and facial expression.

Her name is Shard. I don't think I can describe her accurately. Though I have never cared for cameras, and have a lifelong aversion to being photographed myself, I do regret refusing to bring a camera. Someday I will long for a photograph of her absurd and exquisite beauty. Typical of the Borsogan, she has no more fat on her body than a young sapling. Her legs are long and her buttocks small. Her eyes are far apart, as are her breasts; I can place my whole hand between those small lemon-like mounds. Her gray albino skin is smooth and hairless, as if she were made of mahogany. But it is those unreadable red eyes that rivet my attention. It is not until she smiles or wrinkles her brow that I have the slightest inkling of what she's thinking.

She pounces on me with no modesty or reservation. I must learn to pace myself. Her only demands of me are sexual and I want to please her. She pleases me, especially in that I have the privacy of my thoughts, something I was never able to retain in other marriages. With such a relaxed and simple life, how could we be anything but happy?

March 2
How could I have been fooled? Did I believe my little gray Shard was a naked mountain saint? But she is probably more hurt than me. I was on the verge of hitting my little wife. Her red eyes filled, then overflowed with tears. She didn't bother to wipe them away. She didn't sob. Finally, I took her in my arms. Who am I to resist the force of nature?

March 4
I couldn't take it any longer. I dragged Boccho to Choheh's hut and, sitting in that warm familiar space, poured out my heart, Boccho struggling to keep up with my effusion of woe. When she had heard it all she smiled, looked into my eyes, and spoke.

"I can tell that there are many things you do not know. This is my fault. I should have taken more care with you. But you are a smart man and I thought you knew everything. Also, needing an interpreter for long conversations is irritating, which can cause the food in one's stomach to rot and the mouth to become dry.

"You are upset because you went out to make water and found Shard making the Sun with a ghost. You think you have not been a good husband, but you are wrong. Shard and I have talked. She thinks you are a good husband and she is proud to be your wife. Before she was married, people blamed her for poor fishing, but now everyone thinks that together the two of you have pleased the Sun. Fishing has been good and no women have gone lopsided. At first she was worried about the strange shape of your wanger on the end, but she says it has not been a problem. She says you give her deep feelings when you make the Sun together.

"You see, once a woman stops making babies, when the blood of the Sun stops coming out of her, she has to send her husband away. He becomes a man of the Moon—a ghost. At night the ghosts wander around the village quietly and when women come out to make water they plead with them. The women feel sorry for the ghosts and make the Sun with them. But they do not lie down with ghosts. They must do it standing up. Many women do what you saw Shard doing.

"The ghosts are very sad creatures, but they have a purpose. If a woman's husband dies, the ghosts can keep her happy. And they are old men. What harm can they do? But a few husbands are like you. They are jealous and don't let their wives go out at night. Other husbands have grown tired of their wives and don't care what they do. And some believe that if they let their wives care for the ghosts, when it comes their time to wander the night they will be taken care of."

"But they can make a woman pregnant," I said. Boccho chuckled and passed this statement on to Choheh with a smile. She looked from me to him, her disbelief as obvious as my own at what I'd just heard.

"Women cannot get babies in the night. The Moon has no power in this way. The Sun lets the woman know when it is time for her to have a baby. He stops the blood. Then the man and wife stay home during the day and the husband spits for the Sun as many times as he can and the woman becomes pregnant. And the Sun never fails to make the baby."

I had to look away for a moment. What ignorance! That the Borsogan believed physical and personality traits of the mornicsum could be seen in the mentee's children was one thing. But to believe that women could only be impregnated during the day? And that insemination occurred after the woman's period stopped? Poor Sun, to be the object of such misdirected worship. And to think that I had begun to fall for this anthropological comedy. These old ghosts were probably the fathers of half the children in the village. There was no accuracy of lineage here. How could I tell them that they were playing genetic roulette?

Of course the Sun was successful at making babies after the period stopped. The woman was already pregnant! And there was always a chance that the father was one of the exiled ghosts wandering around late at night with a geriatric hard-on.

I returned my gaze to hers, nodding in my new understanding of the reality of family life, and smiled as if she had given me great comfort. She sighed and smiled with the satisfaction of a job well done—happy to have rescued me from the burden of my ignorance.

When I rose to leave, she hugged me for a long time. She asked that I never tell the Nomtissa that she had done such a poor job as my mornicsum, failing to tell me about the ghosts of the Moon. I promised, of course, and took my leave. Actually, I would rather have stayed with her that night. But I am a husband with duties to perform.

March 7

Shard and I have been building our own hybrid language as we go, but we made a quantum leap forward discussing the incident with the ghost. We sat facing each other for the better part of a day, constructing with words and gestures a bridge between our worlds. I came to believe that she could not have understood my feelings of betrayal, and is truly sorry for the pain she caused.

She has resolved not to respond to the ghosts. I will go out with her when she makes water at night. My respect for my young bride has deepened. But now that we've grown close, I am sure she is older than most Borsogan newlywed brides—perhaps in her early twenties. My theory is that when no mornicsum wanted her charge to marry this gray girl, she was somehow kept secret from the Sun even when her first period was long past. And when the entity in the sky discovered the secret, perhaps she withheld fish. That's when I came into the picture. Now, with Shard married, everything is in balance.

March 8
Heavy rains. No fishing. We eat, rest, and make love.

March 9
Still raining. Last night Shard woke me when she had to make water. We ventured into the downpour laughing and holding hands. She found a place in the grass and squatted, still holding my hand. Out of the corner of my eye I saw something move to our left. Squinting through the rain, I made out the hunched form of a ghost perhaps twenty yards off. I recognized his posture. He was a respected boat builder, relegated, by his age, to advise and direct the work of younger men. But here he was in the rain—a forlorn, aged man of the Moon, awaiting the mercy of urinating women.

Back in our hut, Shard dried our bodies and nestled against my chest. She sighed a sweet, contented sigh and fell to sleep. Things were perfect.

If I stay with the Borsogan, one day I might be a man of the Moon, a ghost of the meadow. But I will likely be dead by the time Shard reaches menopause. Nonetheless, at that moment, I felt the immense isolation of my dying self, adrift in a transient universe.

March 19
The rain has stopped, and the sky has cleared, but I write beneath a cloud. It descended the other evening when I saw the ghost in the rain, Shard squatting beside me in the midnight meadow, the gurgle of her urine in the grass barely audible in the rain. Is my standing between her and this merciful custom really fair?

Then there is death to consider. The peace and harmony of my life compels me to accept it now, along with the poignant realization of how little one life contains—possibility is infinite, our capacity finite. And when I leave the mountain, how will I ingratiate myself into the petty and frantic life I left in America?

I've grown so distraught contemplating these things that Shard fetched Choheh last night. Choheh was reassuring, yet, sensing the depth of my despair, suggested we climb the mountain and see the Nomtissa. Shard was delighted. What a wonderful one she is. Her love has no ambition. My wife in America, by contrast, is ambitious in love and everything else. She is entranced by the vision of the life we should be living. More money, couples' therapy, separate bathrooms, a boat. Shard asks nothing but the hut, our food, the rain, our bodies, and other people likewise involved in living.

March 20
Since there are no mirrors here, I try to keep up the habit of going down to the lake periodically to gaze at my reflection in the water. I don't want to forget what I look like. I hadn't gone for a while, so I went yesterday. But what I saw this time was not I! What stared back at me was an orb of luminous straw, pulsing with veined energy. This, I realized, is what we are beyond our human husks. We are pieces of the Sun hardened into bones and painted with flesh.

The hallucination vanished after a few seconds, but what replaced it was just as alarming: a skinny naked man with enormous eyes, wild red hair, and a tangled beard staring back at me, his jaw agape. What happened to the body I knew, to the mind that inhabited that common form? Gone. Swallowed whole by the gulf between two worlds, leaving behind this ghost of straw, this idiot I saw in the water, his posture that of a curious monkey, his schlong dangling between his legs like a midget snake hanging from a tree to peer into the water.

I fell back and staggered away, drunk with absurd clarity, my thoughts coming to me slowly like beats on a deep drum. Yet I cannot call them thoughts. They were realizations, or, rather, a single realization played over and over with different feeling tones each time the drum was struck. I moved in slow motion, observing everything around me—the people, the huts, a little girl sitting on the ground playing with a pile of pebbles—and despite the tolling drum of realization, I was more a part of the world than I ever have been.

I stumbled into my hut and eased myself down onto the mat. I fell asleep and it continued, the same body truth played over and over, each beat with a unique resonance of that truth, until Shard shook me awake, urging me to eat before I went to see the Nomtissa.

It was again a long death march to the Nomtissa's hut, the outer circumference of my soul shorn of vanity and pretense, Choheh and her entourage padding along behind me quietly.

The Nomtissa beamed when he saw us. He nodded at me and sat smiling softly as Choheh passed around the root drink. Boccho took his place next to me, and I hurriedly described my experience by the lake. I explained how the power of the Sun, within me and within everything, was so immense and vital that I could not picture living the life I once had.

Choheh moved forward and began sucking him. It didn't bother me anymore. Boccho had explained to me that the Nomtissa could never have sexual relations in the full sense like the other ghosts, but oral stimulation by an achva was allowed. However, her ministrations seemed to have no effect on him. He focused exclusively on my words.

I continued my diatribe until my angst was spent. When I fell finally silent, he sighed, closed his eyes for a few moments, then gently pushed Choheh away. He sat up straight and breathed deeply. He smiled at me and spoke a few sentences. Boccho turned and clarified in English.

"I know exactly what you mean," he said. "This world is deep and wide. But here is the truth. Everything exists."

There was a long silence in the hut. In unison, we all began to nod. Everything exists. An irrefutable truth. Simple, inevitable and all encompassing. Everything exists.

On the way back down the hill, Shard, Choheh and I walked with our arms around one another, smiling the idiot smiles of wisdom. We were recipients of a wonderful gift. Everything had changed.

March 24
Much rain.

March 31
The word has come down that the Sun told the Nomtissa I should work with the ghosts making new boats. Constructing these grass canoes is the chief function of the ghosts (besides being the secret fathers of half the village). I've always loved boats and spent a lot of time canoeing as a boy. In fact, I once canoed down the Ohio River with my father. Today, however, was my first day, so I just watched them as they worked.

April 2
Today I braided some reeds for the boats. It was a simple task. I made a few suggestions, simple things the Borsogan would never think of that might eliminate some duplication of effort. They nodded and incorporated the suggestions immediately. I even got one smile of thanks. But I'm the one doing most of the learning. It still amazes me that a canoe can be made of grass.

April 15
I have less and less to write. I am a boat-maker. Who am I

writing for, anyway? Myself? How useful can that be? Besides, I only have one pen left. When it runs out of ink I won't be able to write at all.

May 25

I stopped writing for a month and some days, and it was easy. Does writing catch fish? What good is it anyway? When I return home can I show my American wife these scribbles about my albino wife? Maybe I'll leave the journal here with people who cannot read. Or burn it. But if this tattered notebook has somehow found its way into your hands, dear reader, I have news.

Shard is pregnant! Her periods have stopped and Choheh, delirious with happiness, ordered me to stay home and "make the baby" now that the Sun has stopped Shard's bleeding. My rational mind knows this is needless; she's already pregnant. Yet I go about my duty diligently. I also know the baby cannot be mine. I had a vasectomy eight years ago. The father can only be a ghost.

May 30

One of the ghosts, the one I suspect is the father of Shard's baby, has died. He told us, his fellow boat-makers, that he was going to die as soon as we finished the boat we were working on. We knew it was true. There was a light in his eyes, as if he was seeing the peaceful dark at the end of the tunnel, but he was still vibrant. And he kept tramping about at night pleading with the women who get up to make water.

So when the crooked ghost didn't to come to work, we went to the ghost hut and found him dead. The Nomtissa came down and proclaimed his death a good one. There were no signs of foul play by the Moon. That evening there was a celebration with food and dancing. People gathered in groups and talked about him with obvious respect. His body was on a mat near the water's edge with stones tied to his ankles.

Finally, as the Sun came up, the Nomtissa rowed the body far out on the center of the lake and rolled it into the water. The Sun will have the fish eat his earthly remains, I'm told. And so for two days, no one will fish so the Sun can give the crooked ghost her full attention.

June 1
I walk home at the end of the day with the other boat-makers. We amble along naked, silent, and ready for a nap before the evening meal. Shard comes out to greet me, a little plump now with the baby of a ghost and a smile that makes gray the warmest color on the spectrum. I could live happily to the end of my days here. Of course, I would eventually become a ghost, but that might not be a bad retirement—wandering about at night making love with young women.

Yet it is time for me to leave. I am returning a year late from my "little recreation," as my wife calls my expeditions. I've been late before, but never a year. We have an agreement: no letters while I'm gone. "Out of sight, out of mind," she says as she kisses me at the train station and walks away. Though I seldom think of her, she flows in my blood. Perhaps I am the same for her, though her blood may be boiling by now.

What does she look like? What books has she read? Did she get the tenured position? New friends? She collects friends like an old woman collecting teacups, and she complains to them endlessly about her marriage. They sympathize with her, and I feel their cool glances at faculty teas. Such a woman does not deserve to be married to a shiftless, wandering con artist—poor woman!

June 15
In a month, another walking party will arrive. When they leave, after a short visit, I will go with them. I am going home. Preparing to leave, my mind works and adjusts without me. Out of nowhere, I remember the route to the dry cleaners from our house. I wonder who will be Shard's next husband.

Our marriage has found her favor with the Sun. She has become, for lack of a more appropriate word, popular—as close to a celebrity as her culture allows. I suspect there was more apprehension about my staying here for a year than I knew. But our marriage and her pregnancy put that to rest. My guess is that Shard will be a coveted mornicsum when she is older—a woman of unusual experience, capable of tutoring even the strangest and most difficult of young men.

I, on the other hand, may find that my wife has divorced me and is married to some idiot professor specializing in the study of Dickens. I have always hated Dickens and that would be her departing slap in the face to me. She brings up Dickens at gatherings when she wants to make me squirm. But, if she is still mine, I will make it up to her. She is a treasure. What if she has sold the house and moved to another city? Would I still have the skills to survive in the Western world without her?

What has happened politically? What movies have been made? What fashions? And my sister and her husband, those useless academic bloodhounds—will they still sit cloaked in arrogance and bombast in front of the television, eating ice cream and passing judgment on the world? And my Kafka-obsessed nephew? He has some promise, if I can just talk him out of going to college. Fat chance of that. I am the only fish in my family who has jumped out of the school.

June 22
Today, I am at a loss.

July 1
American dreams creep into my sleep. Last night, an army of men with swords marched naked into an unparting sea and were drowned. Suddenly, I was at a football game with Shard, whom I lost in the crowd. As the game ended, I realized I had watched the game on TV. Then—there on the screen—

was Shard urinating on the grass near our hut. Part of an insurance commercial, as it turned out.

July 3
The walking party has arrived! I am going home in a few days. It is almost morning and I've been too excited to sleep. There are two Americans with the party. I was stunned to hear someone call out in English as I sat down by the lake while we were taking a break. I turned around to see a dark-haired woman in synthetic exercise clothes walking toward me.

I had not seen a Western woman in so long, I stood starring at her. She beamed a wide, motherly smile as she hurried in my direction. When the distance between us was closed, we gaped at one another for several seconds. I was unnerved to notice her enlarged breasts, puffed up with silicone, protruding from her zip-up polyester shirt.

In the meanwhile, the boat-makers simply got up and returned to work after a few half-curious glances. As they sauntered by, I saw them as an American would. Their curious detachment that had so beguiled me upon first seeing them returned for an instant.

Then I hugged this woman. That was a mistake. I think she misread my intent—my being naked and all. For me, there was no hint of sexuality in the gesture. Her implants pressed into me like carved stone and I found myself repulsed by their foreignness.

Her name is Gwen. We talked for hours here in the hut as Shard fed us. I explained, with great difficulty, the relationship between Shard and myself. Gwen wanted to take pictures but I refused the request. That would be tantamount to theft somehow. She said that her son, the other American, had a video camera. I will see that he does not use it. The Sun would withhold fish if it were to be used here. And if her son showed them moving images of themselves it would make the women lopsided. Cameras are of the Moon. But he is asleep now, as is his mother. I hear her breathing.

She almost died when Shard sat down beside me, reached between my legs, and started stroking my member as if it was a pet. Genital petting is so common here, I take it for granted, but Gwen's cheeks shone red and she turned away.

English tasted so good in my mouth, but the hut is silent now and I go to Shard. She is waiting. I can see her red eyes glowing in the dark.

July 11
I am gone. It was easier to leave than I imagined. Shard gave me food and held my hands to her beautiful swollen belly, and then she kissed my eyes. Though there were no promises, I know she believes I will return, as men often go on long walks—gone for weeks or months. My young wife will be safe here to the end of her days. I asked Choheh to explain things more completely to Shard, but she shrugged off the request. She, too, thinks I will return. But perhaps she will explain things to Shard after I've been gone for a while. Widows and widowers do often marry here, with little fanfare. Shard will be fine. She will remember me as the husband of her youth.

Choheh said the Nomtissa might come down to say goodbye, but he didn't show. I nodded farewell to those we met on the way out of the village—that is all. But my feelings were not hurt by the lack of sendoff. There is so little sentimentality at this altitude. People don't dwell on what is gone or lacking, unless it is fish.

Now we're camped at the foot of the rim. Tomorrow we climb. This will be my last entry—writing would disturb the mindset I need to prepare for reassimilation. I still walk with the dreamy intent of the mountain people, but I am clothed now, and these pants and shirt inoculate my body with the ideas of civilization. Yet I'm filled with a completeness for which there are no precise English words. Though I can't capture it in this language, I know the source of this feeling. It is what the Nomtissa told me: everything exists.

POLLEN

William Hayworth looked past her, as the blind will do.

"I am here," she said, "to make sure you are not forgotten."

He tilted his head slightly, as if to hear more clearly what she would say next. She did not speak again right away, though, as she continued to study him. His skin was remarkable for a man nearing eighty. True, flesh drooped beneath his chin and creased in deep parentheses around his mouth, but the visual feel of the epidermis lacked the tissue-thin quality of the truly elderly. She supposed he took good care of his skin. It was endearing that he had retained his vanity. Perhaps, being blind, vanity came easier as he was free from the falsity of mirrors.

Was it this tenacious vanity that enabled him to keep a harem—none of whom he could see?

He could, of course, touch the women. He could feel their beauty. She had been warned about his touching, but was undaunted by his legendary lechery. She was here to witness his life, blemishes and all, and she was proud to do it. Besides, he'd already touched her, seduced her, with his writing, long ago.

His book, *Always a Stranger*, was the first great piece of literature she'd read. It touched her even now, though she could see he was no longer the man who had written *Always a Stranger*. Nor was she the sixteen-year-old girl, naked beneath her limp, warm sheets, entwined with his long passages of beauty. *Stranger* groomed her, seduced her, and lured her into the dangers of the world. Oh, but those days were gone, weren't they? She had long ago sacrificed the innocence required to be the ideal reader she once was. She was backstage now with the ropes and curtains of language, the phantom actors of memory and neurosis, the horror of personal solitude and loneliness—the blood of one's own writing.

She came now, as an adult, to stand toe-to-toe with him: two writers in the world of 2045 that increasingly underappreciated their art. Ironically, perhaps, that world was, in the deepest way, authored by them.

Language forms the world, and as Harold Bloom had intoned, "Shakespeare invented personality." William Hayworth had invented something, too. In a world intoxicated with virtual experience, he stood for the visceral, the sensual, and the chaotic. He brought back the importance of the body as the outer circumference of the soul. That had been the quote in the front piece of *Always a Stranger*: "The body is the outward circumference of the soul." —William Blake. Everything William Hayworth wrote thereafter was rooted in this belief, and what had initially seemed to critics and readers an anachronistic, romantic notion had impregnated her with a fascination with the work and the man who wrote it, though he was already in his thirties in 2008 when the first edition of *Stranger* was published. She'd read it years later, after the critics, and the readers, had come around.

Now, here he was. And here she was, waiting for his

response. It was as they said: "You will have to wait for him to speak."

Was his silence due to his photographic memory and his blindness? This human encyclopedia of emotion, intellect, and art—must he categorize everything and visualize it before releasing it to the seeing world?

His detractors, after the harem publicity, claimed he'd suffered a stroke. Hugh Hefner did it back in the last century, but Hefner, after all, was a dealer in slick porn, not a significant literary figure. It was a silly thing for an old man to do, the harem. "It is beneath the greatest author in our post-masculinist age to indulge in such brute and vain sexual behavior," one wrote. "This is 2045, not 1978."

But wasn't it understandable, she argued (in the private arena of her own inner dialogue), for a wealthy man, adored for the greater part of his life, to take up some eccentric activity to energize the spirit of his glory, as the passage of time led him toward the veils between this world and the next? The truth of this man's life had not yet been told, but as his biographer, she would be the one to provide something more revealing and pure than the treatment other writers had given him thus far.

William Hayworth sighed and nodded but did not speak. His long, delicate fingers rested on lanky legs sheathed in black pants of a fabric she could not identify: not silk, not cotton, and like no synthetic fabric she knew. Another of his eccentricities was that he had a tailor. Who knew there were tailors anymore? Most people had their clothes made, it was true, but the Blue Tube could accomplish the construction of custom clothing so efficiently, it seemed a little silly for an old man to have his clothing pieced together from swaths of fabric in such a primitive way. Yet there was an elegance to it, as there was to everything Hayworth did. How did he accomplish this? In his fiction, it was the precision of his work, and the infinite patience he took with every nuance. So perhaps she, too, should be more patient. Let him be silent. She would wait.

She heard a sound. What was it? Then she recognized it: snoring. The man who sat before her in the rapturous leather chair was snoring. She was stunned. Beyond that, she was hurt. How long had she prepared for this? How hard had her agent worked, and how patient had they been with his requests and questions concerning everything about her? They laughed when he requested photographs—he was blind, for Christ's sake! They had discussed how he might have one of his harem girls describe what she looked like. That was when her agent had warned her not to let him believe she was going to be one of his girls. "It might be tempting, and you could probably sell your book easily if you were sleeping with him, but don't even think about it. It would be disgusting."

But of course she had thought about it—how could one not, knowing who he was? And she had dismissed it. If he were forty, she would not have hesitated for an instant. She had fantasized about it, immersed in his language on those damp onanistic Saturday mornings. But time had buried that particular eclipse of the heart into the trillion-fold compost of things that were fated not to happen.

Besides, soon she would be married to The Idiot and have The Idiot's child, because that was what she had chosen. Of course, The Idiot was adorable, but he was as illiterate as a monkey. And when she told him so, he hadn't really known what illiterate meant. "I can damn well read!" As intelligent and successful as he was, he had no idea of the scholastic definition of that word. But wasn't that the state of things? Who read? Who cared? The mess the Internet had made of reading at the turn of the century always left her wishing she'd been born in the 1960s. The Blue Tube tripled the effect. And movies, too, were horrible—she refused to watch anything made after 2015. For holographic movies she had no use. Why walk around in the story? People were so distracted they could comprehend no plot or substance. The literary elements of film had fallen away. Nothing but the damn Blue Tube remained.

What should she do? She was willing to wait for him to wake up, but that would set a precedent. He might then feel he could fall asleep any time during their interviews—and, well, he could, but was that any basis for a working relationship? Was she to sit and wait while he snored? Certainly she was not his equal in this arrangement, but was she his servant?

Yes, she was. Who was she, after all? A writer, sure, but an unknown one—one who had, in fact, practically begged to be his servant. When finally the deal was struck, she remembered going to a restaurant and sitting alone watching others eat and talk, chattering and bobbing their heads like mechanical monkeys—sipping, chomping, and manipulating their masks with all the poses of response and aggression called for in this particular social situation—and thinking that none of these people would ever experience what she was going to experience. None of them would ever know William Hayworth personally. They might read her biography of him, they might read the stories he would dictate to her, but they would never have the thrill of engaging directly with his mind.

"How are your bowels?"

So startling were the words and the voice, so clear and sonorous, that she looked around the room thinking someone else had entered. But it was he. The snoring had stopped. The silence following his words was immense.

"What?"

"How are your bowels?"

"My bowels?"

"Yes, my dear, your bowels. Your feces, your shit, your poop, your droppings. Because I will tell you this: nothing is more important than proper elimination. So much attention is paid to what we take in, but so little to how and what we put out. 'An army,' one of Faulkner's characters remarked, 'operates on its bowels.' I really don't know precisely what he meant by that. Faulkner was not inclined to explain every nuance, because his writing—to a heroic degree— was all nuance. When we let all details exist simultaneously, everything becomes nuance. Once you realize, for example, that what you leave behind when you squat is as important as what you eat, dietary wisdom is simplified. Here's the distinction: we eat in groups, but we shit alone. It is because we hate solitude that most people die with five to ten pounds of fecal matter compacted in their intestines. You die alone and full of shit. Sad, isn't it? But I can tell you this: when you are sad, you are closest to the truth. And that is the truest thing I will tell you, and the saddest."

He yawned. "So how are your bowels, dear?"

"Regular."

"Well, regular is far too vague. But you are young and I don't expect candor. You still have hope. You still believe that the time for you to express yourself completely and honestly lies in the future. You imagine that there is a time other than the present in which things will be different and you will emerge the hero of your own life. But you are not the hero of your life. The story of your life doesn't even have characters, let alone heroes."

He yawned again. He had lovely teeth for an old man.

"My diet is reasonable," she said. I've had all my systems analyzed. I know what my body requires. I get my infusions every month. Therefore I would assume my poop is just fine."

"I see. Are you ready then to take dictation?"

"I would like to discuss our working relationship first. I'd like to know how we plan to proceed."

He nodded, pursed his lips, and drummed his manicured fingers on his thigh. "Well, I can tell you how I intend to proceed. I don't know that there is a 'we' in the plan. I thought all the details had been worked out. I thought it was perfectly clear that you would take dictation and then—

then, meaning subsequently—I would roll out the details of my life so that you could compile a biography. But I could be wrong. The agreement could have been that you come to my home and bully me with your sightedness and passive-aggressive manipulations into revealing my soul, so that I become a helpless old man exploited by the imagined vitality of your youth. Perhaps that was the agreement."

"What?"

"Never mind. I am sorry. Never grow old, my dear. It makes you mean and resentful. And you can imagine how much worse I would be if I didn't have healthy bowels and a good dentist. Now, where were we? Ah, the working arrangement. Well, I suggest I give you my first story—it is quite brief—and the next time we meet, we will work on the biography."

"That's just fine, Mr. Hayworth. Is that what I should call you? What should I call you?"

"You can call me William, or Old Fuck Knuckle, if you wish."

"William. I'll call you William."

"Yes, yes. William it is. And I will call you Ingenue. Now the story: 'Buoyant.'"

Ingenue reached into her purse, took out her computer and unfolded it. "I'm ready."

He took a deep breath, smiled, and raised his hands before him, flexing his fingers in the direction of the massive window on the other side of the room, as if to take the light in through his hands.

"I do love to write," he said, with such warmth and sweetness that her heart jumped and she almost reached out to touch his arm.

"Originally 'Buoyant' was in first person. I prefer writing in first person, yet each story dictates itself to me in a different fashion. Here, third person is best. And so we begin."

At some point, he realized there was a problem. He was dead. Conventional wisdom has it that beyond death there are no problems, and this would include the problem of one's death. The falsity of this truism was his first epiphany. The second was that he still had a body and continued to walk and talk among the living, who showed no sign of recognizing his new condition.

Certainly his wife did not notice. Each morning, she planted her coffee-flavored kiss on his lifeless lips as she hurried, phone in hand, out the door and down the walk to the light-rail station a few blocks from their brick suburban bungalow, with no indication in her demeanor to acknowledge a dead spouse.

But it was after her departure that his condition imposed itself more forcefully. His bones dissolved, he floated upward like a helium balloon, and for the rest of the day he would bob like a buoy at the mercy of the air currents of his home. If the heater came on he might be buffeted about in the hallway for several minutes. This was a shock in the beginning, but he soon learned to recognize the clicking sound the thermostat made just before the furnace kicked in and so was able to brace himself for the swift force of the warm air.

Other things could not be anticipated. One breezy day, his wife left a window open in the spare room and he was pinned in the corner above the television for three hours. But for the most part, his was a pleasant death, conducive to napping and a variety of hypnagogic states during which the mundane articles of his home became animated and spoke to him. The couch became a French-speaking leopard, for example, and the blender spoke in a singsong trill like a kindergarten teacher. While he had no control over where he might float, he was able to control, to a certain degree, whether or not he napped or half-napped, and thus could choose between various internal environments, from light dozing to deep sleep, unhampered by the judgments and self-recriminations of the living.

Most baffling was this: to his dreaming self, his waking self was a dream. His dreams, like those of a living person, might contain elements of his waking life, such as his wife or his cat, but more remarkable was the fact that his waking life contained the elements of his dream life in exactly the same way. In indistinct states between the extremes, all elements were activated. In any case, these things hardly mattered, since he was dead.

His wife, a habitual creature, came through the door each evening at 5:35, give or take a few minutes. If awake, he deflated at the sound of her key, welcomed her at the door with a kiss, inquired about her day, and poured her a glass of wine while she flossed her teeth, and donned her robe and slippers. He assumed this ritual remained the same when she arrived while he was sleeping, since she would have noticed any break in routine. She would also have noticed any decrease in his production. But each day he gave her fresh pages and she toiled over them while he fixed dinner. She sipped her wine, grunted, twirled a lock of her hair around her little finger, and tattooed his pages with red ink. Her editing complete, they ate while she talked.

"I can't believe anyone could be so incompetent. I told her exactly what I wanted, but when she showed me, everything was out of order. I could have saved time and money by hiring the whole thing out. It's not my fault she has problems. I told her, 'Look, the work world is not built around your personal life.' Seven years. I cannot believe it has been seven years."

Later, they read in the living room, listening to the Bulgarian Women's Choir or a Belizean flautist named Beliza Perdomo. He might glance over the pages, discounting a major portion of her edits, cursing her in his thoughts while she read and sipped a second or third glass of wine.

On Thursday evenings, they watched a television show, but each night at eleven o'clock she announced her intent to "go beddy-bye," and with her yawning departure, their evening together would end and he'd inflate once more to bob above the television, perhaps eying the unwashed dishes or the television itself, with its flat babbling face, as he slipped into his dreams. He might wake at some point to find the television off and the dishes done. Or he might dream that he was making love to the familiar warmth of his wife. Often it was her dreamy moans of pleasure that woke him, but he did not mind the interruption of his inner life that copulation demanded.

Yet he was troubled. He had wished for a death more exciting to deliver him from the dishes and unwanted edits. Like all victims of psychology, he longed for resolution and closure. And the effort required to keep writing seemed too much to ask of the dead. Eventually, however, his problems were solved in one fell swoop.

His wife died quietly in her sleep of a previously undiagnosed heart ailment described in the autopsy as "advanced angina." He did not remember the event, even though it took place a few inches from him, since he was asleep and dreaming above her. She did not die in his dreams, but asleep in her own.

The funeral was sad and glorious. He had no idea his wife's editorial talents were so valued beyond the confines of her work on his own manuscripts. For the first time, he met writers he'd admired for decades who praised her work, in some cases on books he had read without realizing she had worked on them. How sad, he thought, that I didn't get to know her better before I died.

When finally the tears of ritual were shed and dried and she was planted in the earth, he returned to his routine and found things were not as different as he might have imagined. It was true that he bobbed about in the drafts of the house for longer periods without the grounding of his wife's stale, caffeinated kiss, but now his writing was completed, like the dishes and the dusting, by segments of himself he could not remember. And that, he decided after a few months, was fine. That he was still writing made him feel stoic and useful—vital, in fact. What more could a dead man ask?

~

William chuckled and closed his eyes. Ingenue folded her computer slowly and slipped it into the pocket of her sweater, nodding to herself. Glancing up, she thought he had fallen asleep again, but he turned his head in her direction, as if he could see her.

"That was 'Buoyant.'"

"It was. . ."

"It was what?"

"I don't know. It has a sad grace to it. Aptly titled, to be sure. I like it."

"I like it, too," he said. "Now, next time we'll work on your book, but enough for now."

"Will someone show me out?"

"I don't know," he replied softly, sleep already overtaking him. "See if you can find someone."

She paused in the hallway, yearning to see a member of the harem, but was approached instead by a young pregnant housekeeper who spoke no English, but smiled excessively to make up for it.

Walking across the drive to her antique Tesla, she sniffed the air, feeling sixteen and alive. Why? Not exactly because of William, she decided, but because things could be created. Everything was created. The world was a creation. Tonight she could make love to The Idiot with a clear conscience, because she had performed something of herself today. She had opened the frozen door of her inner library and walked through an ageless sunset at the side of a man who was himself almost buoyant. She was speaking with death and it was alive as ever. The Idiot would be so happy with her. She would defer to him in conversation, she would listen, and, finally, in the cool, circular grayness of their bedroom, she would undress slowly, watching the boyish glee in his eyes and the rise of his member, whom he called Hector, as it bobbed its beef-hearted head, regaining consciousness, beat by idiot heartbeat.

Her bones hummed with power as she steered down the winding road with the windows down, away from William's mansion.

"Was 'Buoyant' a response to some event in your own life, William?"

He was restless in his chair today, crossing and uncrossing his legs, smoothing his pants, caressing the large brown leather arms of the chair. Perhaps he'd had a good night's sleep, perhaps a frisky morning with the harem. He wore a green silk shirt with cuff links of knotted leather and an even larger pair of dark glasses than he'd worn in their first session.

He pressed his fingertips together and cocked his head in thought. Though she knew it was silly, she mimicked him. She'd read that, in conversation, if one reflects the posture and gesture of the other party, that party is unable to resist confiding in the unconscious mirror you have created. She hoped her posture would somehow be conveyed in her voice and that his blindness would not hinder the effect, that he would be able to sense how her body was dancing with his.

"Well, I have not died yet, if that's what you mean."

They shared a chuckle. He smiled in her direction and nodded a silent approval that spread through her blood like opium. He was her father, she knew, in the literary sense. There might be others who felt this, but she alone sat with him in his mansion with the history of his life about to unfurl between them.

"But it is based rather loosely on my second wife, a woman who adored picking blueberries as much as she did making love. Ah! No, wait. That's the next story I'm going to dictate. The story 'Buoyant' came from a dream of dying, with some fragments—especially the part about her job and the coffee-flavored kiss—related to my fourth wife, who was, incidentally, my editor during a difficult period. I'd lost confidence in my method, so I took to doing several rewrites of everything. What a waste. If you write slowly, you don't need anything but a few polishing passes before you publish."

"I noticed you spoke slowly as you dictated, and you never had me go back to correct anything."

"Yes. I have the auditory equivalent of a photographic memory. Like a composer, I hear and revise in my head before I write or speak—now that I have your lovely feminine presence to assist me—and that is how it is done."

"I'm envious."

"You should be. But I am envious of you, as well. You have so many more lives to live in the life you have been given. I'm seeing the dark at the end of the tunnel."

"But you are far from done, William."

He smiled. "So where do we begin with the story of my life? It indeed will be a story. We live only by story, and story is a human construction. Trees do not live by stories, as far as we know. Ever tell a story to a dog? Brilliant as they are, they are oblivious to us prattling on. They know when you speak of going for a walk or feeding time—most definitely they understand when you tell them you love them. But for your stories they have no use. And who can blame them? Each time we tell a story, whether it is the epic of how long you waited for service in a restaurant or the history of the Roman Catholic Church, you take yourself and the listener out of the present moment. Ultimately, what is the use of that? But we have no choice. We live in a semantically created universe. We might as well enjoy the story. And as long as we understand that no story—especially the story of one's life—is ever true, then we are just fine."

"But in your essays, you say that truth comes through myth. So if we live by story, or by mythologizing everything, then are we not living by truth?"

"Truth with a capital 'T' comes through myth. But that sort of truth has nothing to do with actuality, or verifiable truth in the scientific sense. It is a kind of intuitive truth. There is nothing true about Jesus, even though he speaks the Truth. None of the men who wrote the gospels were ever in his presence. And those third-hand stories were edited and coaxed into forms that suited the troop of papal shamans who practiced political priest-craft over the centuries. The gospels are not the true accounting of actual events, yet the Truth of his teachings is still with us. That is Truth coming through mythology. Jesus leads us to the great intuitive Truth that we have within us—so deep and mysterious that the intellect cannot comprehend or contain it. Just as the Truth the Buddha speaks is within us in the form of our Buddha Nature."

"So all religious organizations miss the point?"

"They do not miss it, they contain it like a glass contains the wine. They contain the mystery for the succeeding generations so that it might be imbibed. But often they come to feel, these organizations, that they are indeed the wine itself. So they speak as if they are God or the Buddha. Best to ignore them and drink the Truth unpolluted. After all, these functionaries are responsible only for the glasses, not the wine."

"But aren't we responsible for bringing this 'truth' to others, then?"

"There's an old saying: 'You can lead a horse to Truth, but he will refuse to get drunk.' Ultimately, you can't help anyone. When you try, it is often because you want to prove yourself or achieve some exalted goal you have set for yourself. It is vanity. You have mistaken yourself for wine when you are only the glass. If someone wants your help, they can ask. If they don't ask, leave them alone."

"That just seems so selfish."

"Let me dictate a story, one I have had for some time. It will explain this idea and will suffice as the story of the beginning of my life, which occurred when I was thirty or so."

"Your life began when you were thirty?"

"A story must begin somewhere. After all, we have an eternity behind us and ahead of us. Where we begin the story is entirely up to us, as we are the fiction we live. Give me a moment."

He rocked side to side for a minute, then continued rocking for nearly half an hour. Finally, he said, "Next time," and fell asleep.

As she left, she thought she heard the crying of babies— not just one or two babies, but many babies. The pregnant housekeeper winked at her and smiled goodbye.

When she returned a week later, William began to deliver the story with no prelude, as if she had just left the room for a few moments.

~

The runner ran without a torch, naked and with his eyebrows shaved. His destination was the home of an old man who examined young runners to determine whether or not they were worthy of receiving a torch.

As the runner passed through the advancing partitions of nights and days, his feet grew sore and his legs weaker and weaker. But he continued at his steady pace, cherishing the pain and fatigue, for these were signs that his run was a worthy one.

After seven days, he came within sight of the old man's round stone house. Seeing the house made him realize, all at once, how long he had been running and how much he feared facing the old man. He began to lag, gasp, and clutch his side.

Suddenly, he was at the door. Exhausted, he sank to his knees. Though he had not knocked, an extremely tall woman in silk robes opened the door. Her huge blue-green eyes shed steady rivulets of tears, and in her left hand she held a wooden crucifix the size of a baseball bat.

She sighed mournfully and motioned him through the door with the cross. She bent and sang softly to him, her voice trembling with emotion. "You think you're the only one, don't you? You think you're the only one, don't you? No, you are not the only one to think you are the only one. No, you are not the only one to think you are the only one." Then, drawing herself up to her full height, she motioned for him to follow her down the hallway.

The hallway emptied into a stone-walled spiral staircase and she let him pass to go up the stairs, the top of his head brushing the underside of her breasts as he did. He turned to thank her, and just in time, for she shrieked and swung the crucifix at his head with all her might. He ducked and the cross whistled by, exploding in splinters against the wall.

In his panic, the runner leapt up the stairs two at a time for several minutes and would have kept on if he had not heard two voices behind him calling, "Hey, wait for us!" from an adjoining hallway. He stopped and waited cautiously, ready to take flight at the sight of the tall silk woman. Instead, a man and a different woman came around the corner, both naked with shaved eyebrows in the tradition of runners.

"You don't have to worry up here," the woman said. "She can't come on the stairway."

The man held out his hand and introduced himself and his wife as retired runners who worked for the old man as stairway keepers.

"Have you been a runner long?" asked the man.

"Nearly all my life."

"And you're here to get a torch?" the woman asked.

The runner nodded.

The woman pinched the skin of her abdomen as she spoke; it was covered with red welts.

"Please keep your eyes off my wife's body," the man whispered in the runner's ear.

"Touch my stomach," his wife whispered in the other. The runner turned and moved up the stairway. The couple caught up immediately and kept him between them as they continued. The runner kept his pace quick and was silent.

After several minutes, the woman leaned her head forward and, looking past the runner, said to her husband. "He's really quite graceful, don't you think?"

The husband was quiet for a few steps before replying, "I can't argue with that. But grace does not imply running talent. I have known people who walked with grace and they are walking still."

The woman laughed.

"You have such a way with words, Jake."

Finally, they reached the last step. Wider and deeper than the rest, it formed a porch for a huge wooden door.

"Is this the old man's room?" the runner asked.

They both nodded. Then, suddenly, powerfully, the woman slammed herself into the runner, trapping her husband between the runner and the wall.

The husband bellowed.

"What's wrong, Jake?" the woman screamed. "Is a man's ass against you too much? Too close to home, Jake?"

The pinned husband reached around the runner and grabbed two handfuls of her hair and shook her head violently.

"Remember your oath," she squealed. "Remember, Jake, remember!"

Jake let go and was silent.

The runner tried to move, but the woman's strength was tremendous.

She put her lips to his ear. "I just had to feel you against my stomach," she whispered.

They stood in this position for several minutes. Then, abruptly, with a giggle, the woman lifted one leg and pushed the wooden door with her foot. It swung open slowly.

In a combined effort, as if the action had been rehearsed, the couple released the runner and flung him through the door onto the stone floor of the room.

As the door closed behind him, he rolled onto his side and moaned. He stood slowly, looking around the bare room. The old man was curled against the wall, sleeping.

"Sir, may I speak with you?"

The old man woke with a start and, jumping to his feet, began trotting around the room. His gait was perfect, his stride smooth, but there was something, perhaps a hint of stiffness in the joints, that betrayed his extreme age.

"Sir, I have come to speak to you about a torch."

The old man ran a couple more times around the room, then said, "You've come to see me about a torch and yet you stand there like a tree. If you're a runner, run!"

"But sir," the runner replied, beginning to trot, "I ran for seven days to get here."

"Seven days is nothing. I used to run for twelve. Why did you even bother me if seven days is the best you can do? You don't really expect a torch for that, do you?"

"Oh, that's not the longest I've run. My best is nine days."

"That's not so bad." The old man had stopped and now sat watching the torch-seeker run around. "Still, nine days is far from great. But there is much more to being a runner than just running, especially when one has a torch. Are you aware of that?"

"Yes, sir. I certainly am."

"Have you studied our history?"

"Yes, I have."

"Then go ahead. Plead your case."

"May I stop running to talk?"

"If you must."

The runner knelt before the old man and said, "Sir, I want a torch so that I can bring light to those who live in darkness."

The old man stared at the torch-seeker for a long moment, then burst out laughing. His laugh echoed in the room, and before the echo died he took another breath and began laughing harder. He bent over with laughter. He tried to raise himself again, but laughter possessed him and curled his body still more. He rolled to his side, howling insanely and beating his palms on the floor. Tears welled in his eyes and the veins of his face bulged. He laughed so hard that he could not close his mouth and drool hung in strings from his lip. He laughed so long that echoes of his laughter began to echo in his laughter. Then, noticing the runner had risen and was turning to leave, the old man managed to stop laughing long enough to point to a stack of unlit torches by the door.

The runner took one as he left.

~

Ingenue crossed her legs. "And that was the beginning of your life?"

"So it is written," he smiled.

She loved the story, yet she'd been tricked. This was his way of avoiding the biography. He promised to tell her the story of his life, then substituted another story. She meant nothing to him. She was a vehicle for his own work, and his promise to her was meaningless.

Her chest tightened, her vision narrowed. She forced

herself to take a deep breath, closed her eyes and tried to fantasize the rage away.

She would take him for a walk, find a cliff, and there hold him from behind and threaten to push him over the edge if he did not tell her the story of his life. The actual events—his parents, his marriages, the love, the sex, the intellectual crises—all of it. But he was blind. He would not see the abyss before him. He lived in an abyss of darkness already. No, she would grab his old penis and pinch it as hard as she could. She would—

"Well, should we begin anew?" he said suddenly.

She opened her eyes. The sun was on his face, and he was handsome for a moment, despite the ravages of age. So this was the man she had loved all these years without knowing him. Perhaps there was nothing extraordinary about him after all. Maybe there was nothing extraordinary about writing. It was a craft, like bricklaying. Writers might be nothing more than technologists of language—just learning the ways, through trial and error, that the mind can be seduced. Pederasts of the spirit. Whores.

"About my early years," he said.

Her heart jumped, and she was ashamed of wanting to push him off a cliff. She was sorry for calling him, in the small theater of her heart, a pederast and a whore. She positioned her fingers above the keyboard. She watched as he raised his face a bit in the light and smiled. Ah, he was indeed handsome. He was beautiful.

"I was the only child in the history of mankind who was older than his parents at the time of his birth."

She took that in for a moment. "You mean you always felt special and your parents couldn't understand you?"

"No. It's an actual fact. When I was born, I was chronologically older than my parents."

"That isn't possible."

"We can't begin the story of my life if you are not

receptive or willing to listen. I speak one sentence and already you bury me with condescension. You say you came so that no one would forget me and you have forgotten me already. You have forgotten everything I said to you from the very beginning. You want to use me. I chose you with great care, and now you turn on me. What have I done to you? You mock my blindness, my clothing, my aging body—"

"I have not! I would never!"

"I can feel it. My bones are dizzy with it. Do you think I don't know that eventually you will interrogate me about my harem? You treat me like a helpless infant. I wanted to be your mentor, to live the life of imagination before your very eyes, but you spit on me. Your disgust for me makes me feel I am being forced to drink the boiling vomit that flows in the rivers of hell."

"You're crazy."

"There! You see? That is it exactly. In your own words. At last you say what you feel about me. I rest my case."

This time she would not go gently into the driveway, down the hill, and back to The Idiot. She stormed by the pregnant housekeeper and into the house. She would find the crying babies. She would interview the harem by force. They would tell her or she would bash their empty heads against the pastel walls.

No one stopped her. From room to room she raged, her hands pumping at her sides, each breath a hoarse croak. If she could not know what it was to write brilliantly, if there were nothing to life but the things of this mundane world, she would rather not live. And him. Let the world forget him. What did she care?

"Can I help you find something?"

The voice was sweet. No other word but sweet could describe it. It was sweet and came from high behind her. She turned to face the breasts of the sweet voice—both the voice and the breasts belonged to the tallest woman she'd ever seen.

She stepped back and lifted her chin to look into eyes large, cold, and green. She swallowed.

"Can I help you with something?"

When the woman spoke, her eyes seemed to soften, but the green of them was still unnerving. Ingenue let her chin fall and again faced the breasts, full and faintly nippled beneath a gossamer beige blouse. "I'm feeling faint."

Long fingers guided her to a couch.

"I understand. I've been feeling faint, too. I'm six weeks pregnant."

"Like the housekeeper?"

"There is no housekeeper. You are the one taking dictation. We've seen you come and go. Your presence has been felt. We assumed you didn't want to meet us, and we've learned not to trust anyone who is a writer."

She looked up into the green eyes. "William is a writer."

"I rest my case."

"He just used that same line."

"He stole it from me. By the way, my name is Lily."

The woman's face verged on beauty when it was still, but looked quite ordinary when her mouth was in motion. The shape of her nose, however, was flawless. It was beautiful beyond the work of any cosmetic surgeon. Possibly, she had the most beautiful nose in the world.

"So you are a member of the harem?"

"There is no harem."

"It's been documented."

"It's been labeled."

"But you aren't the only woman who lives here, are you?"

"I'm kind of the leader."

"Of the women who live here?"

"And many who don't."

"Why do you live here?"

"For the pollen."

Lily's green eyes came closer as she bent down, her lips parting slightly before they met Ingenue's for a kiss as sweet as the voice that had come though them. A tongue more wise and pleading than any tongue or penis she had ever known searched her mouth with such delicacy and care that she fell open mentally, orally, and vaginally as she sank into the couch, unwilling to offer any pretense of protest.

The tall one's long fingers slipped beneath her shirt to caress her breasts, then slithered like a fist of loving snakes beneath her skirt, preparing her for the approach of the tongue that seemed not to have left her mouth before it was between her parting legs, singing like an angel the song that women know precedes the implosion of the rose, the stopping of the mind, and the petite death of tiny contractions pulsing in the very center of the soul's body.

When Ingenue next arrived at the mansion, Lily greeted her at the door with a cup of jasmine tea and a kiss on the top of her head. "Be gentle but firm with him," she advised. "He will abuse patience, but he respects warm resolve. With him, the key is tenderness. Don't argue. Don't debate. You will always lose."

"Can I talk to you when I'm finished with him?"

"You will never be finished with him, and you can always talk to me. Go now. He's expecting you and you want to catch him before he falls asleep."

He was, in fact, nodding off when she entered the room. She went to him and kissed the top of his head, just as Lily had kissed the top of hers. When in Rome. He smiled and tilted his head back as if to see her. "Welcome, welcome." He held up his hand; she took it and squeezed it tenderly.

"I'm glad you're here. I was at work on the new story."

"Oh, did I interrupt you? I'm so sorry."

"No, no. It's fine. I can work any time, but I only get to be with you a few hours a week. Delightful hours, I might add."

He was glowing. Lily had been right—her kiss had transformed him. He was dressed beautifully today. His shirt was chenille, his pants soft denim, and his dark glasses tortoiseshell. Except for the glasses, each article was a different shade of gray, including his quilted silk slippers. She wondered if it was Lily who dressed him, so she asked the question.

"Who is Lily?" he asked with a smile.

"The tall one."

"Remember, I'm blind," he whispered, as if to keep anyone from hearing. She laughed at his joke and he reached out, in the wrong direction, for her to take his hand. She leaned and took the hand, noticing again how firm and warm it was. He was not old at all. He was aged, but he was not old. She could feel the vitality of his blood through the thin veil of skins that separated her blood from his. Now he was the man who had written *Always a Stranger*. This was him. Kindly as a grandfather now, but the vitality was here in her hand. It was as if she was holding his organ, and she blushed inwardly at the thought. He chose this moment to release her hand and take a deep breath.

"I don't mean to be protean in avoiding the biographic material you request," he said sadly. "But one reaches a point as a writer where the memory of what you believed at the time and what you have imagined or written cannot be separated. The writer becomes the written. The author authors himself in order to continue. Once in the ocean, who can tell what water came from which river?"

She unfolded her computer. "We will take it however it comes, William. I ask only that we continue. If the stories are all that is your life, then that is as it is. As I said, I am here to be sure you are not forgotten. How that is to be accomplished, I can't say. But I am resolved."

He smiled so sweetly that her heart ached. This is what

writing was, she thought. It was this surrender to language and emotion, channeled and shaped by the art of years, the deep sex of the mind generating dreams small and specific from the infinity of possibility. It was the writer opening up his being to another. The impersonal personal. Every work is a letter from the writer to the reader. The most public thing and the most private. Nothing could be more intimate. It was even more intimate than what Lily had done with her—or to her. Such a sweet surrender that had been. And now she was surrendering to William, even though, at this moment, she loved Lily more than she had ever loved anyone. But what, she thought in a flash, was she to do with The Idiot? He was expecting to marry her.

"It is called 'In the Aviary,'" William said abruptly. "And it is in first person. I love writing in first person. Here it is—"

~

On their way to the beach, the tourists pass the aviary clutching towels, dragging picnic baskets, and hefting ice chests, loaded with the luggage of their leisure like doe-eyed llamas. Smelling of cocoa butter and snack foods, they draw onward, entranced by the orchestral majesty of the vast blue ocean. The waves surrender to the naked sand in echoing crescendos, the azure infinity of sky jeweled with winging gulls crying out in stabs of ecstasy. And so they pass me by, the old man sitting in the aviary just off the path, witness to their seaward migration, driven by the promise of sun, naked skin, and the warm sands of relaxation.

The island's natives, immune to the enchantment of the sea because of their constant proximity, are even less likely to notice me. So I am left alone with my companions: the moss-green macaws staring with cocked heads as clouds of finches sweep past, the pastel Love Birds grooming each other above the water dishes, the plump English Budgies cracking seeds in their bulldog beaks, impervious to the lilting song of Black-Lipped Guitar Birds clustered together in the branches of their wind-bent perches.

But occasionally, I motion a vacationer closer, just as I did you. I'd have called out to you, but my vocal cords are encrusted with nodes, so all I can manage is this harsh whisper that has you leaning close to hear. But you are intrigued, aren't you? After all, I'm ancient and nearly naked, wearing only a tattered leather loincloth and my beard. But don't I look like a man with a story to tell?

Well, I have a story to tell, so please sit for a few moments and listen, right there on that stump. I will press my face against the cage. There. Now just lean in a little closer and hear my story, the story of a king without a throne. Yes, I am a king. The King of Irony.

The first jewel of irony in my crown is that I, once a talented tenor, should be nearly voiceless in my incarceration here in this birdcage. Beautiful and mindless creatures, the birds mock me day and night with song. But the second irony is far more cruel: my reputation as a rake and a philanderer, which I alternately polished and resisted, has ended with my monogamous enslavement here by a young wife who has locked me (with my permission) in the aviary with her hundred birds, placing upon the gate a lock within my reach that I have never bothered to touch. Nor have I tried to dig beneath the bars and netting to escape. I am more pragmatic than you would imagine—how could a half-mad seventy-year-old wearing a loincloth make an escape anyway? The ferryman would spot me and call to my wife. She would then send the Samoan gardener to fetch me as if I were a dog. Jealous of my marriage as he is, the gardener would find a reason, I'm sure, to shake me like a child or bash my head in with a rock. No one would mourn me but my wife.

But the tale of the third irony—the one I tell you alone, because you have such an honest face—is the most twisted irony. It begins, as most amusing stories do, with pain. In my early thirties, I lived in a cabin at the other end of the island with a tall, skinny girl of twenty.

One evening, we walked to the lake, the marshy nucleus of the island, enjoying the soft breeze and talking of berry picking, for it was blackberry season and our hands and lips were stained with dark juice and our wrists lacerated by bramble.

As we approached the lake, we heard the laughter of loons cavorting in the twilight. Wiser than I, she stayed on solid ground while I crept to the reeded edge, straining so intently to see the loons that I did not hear the buzz of mud hornets upon whose nest I had stepped. In an instant, the kamikaze bastards swarmed me.

Now, to my great misfortune, I was given at the time, at the request of my girlfriend, to walking about with no boxers beneath my shorts, so that she might have quick access to me. The pleasure I had derived from that on multiple occasions, in no way compensated for the wrath of the hornets that flew directly up the loose leg of my shorts and delivered ferocious notice of my trespass.

Within the hour, I was on the cabin bed, writhing in agony and covered with welts the size of scarlet bon-bons. The worst one on the tip of my paralyzed phallus. The envenomed welt was as large as the glans itself, making my penis appear to be crawling out of its own skin, giving birth to a new, redder version of itself.

The girl dabbed me with calamine and kisses, but I could only beg her to kill me.

Finally, subdued by medication, I fell asleep with a full week's recovery ahead. I won't elaborate on how painful urination was during my convalescence—not because I want to spare you, but because I wish instead to detail, without delay, the event that made me capable, to this day, of sustaining sexual intercourse almost indefinitely.

After a few days, my rapacious girl grew restless and, in the process of treating my welts, brought me to a state of arousal extinguishable only by emission. Unfortunately, engorgement made the itching unendurable, and while penetration brought a moment's relief, with copulation came hysteria as I sought to relieve the exponential itching, which was satisfied only by the movement that increased it. The girl cried out in ecstasy and I in agony. Finally, at the apex of our combative frenzy, I climaxed in a screaming ejaculation so excruciating that I lost consciousness.

I'm sure there are those who have experienced pain worse than mine, but I would submit that few have experienced it at the height of intimacy. Imagine a sensation akin to birthing a child through your penis whose end is swollen as hard and tight as a newly stitched baseball. Even today, over fifty years later, the memory makes me twitch.

They say, my young friend, that each moment of our life is registered in our cellular memory; the body's every cell is a sensorium housing the whole of our history as a night holds all our dreams. Our flesh is a living library of our past—this is what the great religion of Psychology teaches. Imagine, then, the intensity of this memory: the post-traumatic stress of a gothic orgasm powerful enough to make a grown man faint. Is it not easy to see how the mind, body, and spirit would conspire in their infinite operational unity to avoid repetition of this event? Psychology would predict impotence here, but Nature swallows such reasonable theories like a teaspoon of sputum tossed into the Grand Canyon. She dictated for me instead a furious libido fueled by an equal fear of ejaculation. The more I feared the impulse to make love, the stronger it became. Once in coitus, the fear of climax postponed that climax to excruciating lengths. So, like the ancient Chinese, (who believed that emission was a loss of essential energy) I developed the art of delaying ejaculation.

But it was not to conserve seminal essence or to prolong

pleasure. My ability to sustain coitus for hours was the child of unconscious dread. It did no good to reassure myself that the torturous orgasm would never reoccur; cellular memory is stronger than reason. And I must confess that my peculiar talent came to dominate the drama I remember as my life. Unlike men, women speak honestly and explicitly to each other about their erotic lives, and news of my endurance brought me collusive fame with the island women.

While I was never wildly promiscuous, I'm sure my adventures as a lover and husband are richer and more complicated than most. I have been worshiped, hated, fought over, and shared like exotic liquor, and I regret nothing—not even my current situation—and will now tell you how I came to be married to my warden, the woman they call Sweet Jane.

Twenty-five years ago, I was a teacher of fifth-graders in the island school and she was the skinny, dark-haired girl who bit me for no apparent reason on her way out the door to recess. With my hand still smarting with the imprint of her young, sharp teeth, I brought her to the principal and we sat with Jane in his office: two grown men bending over her like giants, asking this child why she had sunk her teeth into my hand.

Sweet Jane looked up at us with innocent black eyes and said, "Someday I want to marry him." She was allowed to go without punishment, and we dismissed the incident as a mystery beyond our capacity, though the principal did suggest I clean the wound with alcohol and henceforth keep my hands in my pockets during dismissal.

The island is only seven miles by three and inhabited by only a few hundred people during the tourist off-season, so I watched Sweet Jane grow from girl to teen to woman without noticing her especially, except occasionally to put my hands in my pockets when I saw her approaching along the path to the post office. She was a brown stem of a girl for most of that time, until she seemed to suddenly flower overnight. One day, I saw her and realized the girl was gone and this young woman was the new Sweet Jane.

I heard later that she'd married quickly and badly, and then divorced. She married poorly once again, and after she'd had three daughters, her husband drowned in a fishing accident, which saddened everyone.

She was named Sweet Jane for a reason. Everyone loved her: her eyes could smile without her mouth, and when the full lips joined the deep brown of her laughing eyes, even the most jaded soul walked away grinning like an idiot. Her voice was a clear, inviting flute. She would greet even a stranger like you with a cocked head, a friendly touch, and a charming lift of her delicate brows that suggested the two of you were dearly bound by an ancient shared memory.

So I was not surprised when she took my hand one warm day on the path and held it for a moment between her strong white teeth.

"Do you remember what I said then?" she asked, still holding me captive by the wrist.

"I was in pain," I replied, "I don't remember what happened next."

She laughed, kissed my hand and skipped away. Looking back over her shoulder, she said, "I'll marry you when you're seventy." But I was not alarmed. This was the kind of thing Sweet Jane did to everyone. Besides, I was fifty-one and she was twenty.

But Sweet Jane was true to her word: I was seventy plus eleven days when we married. By then she was a woman of thirty-nine, with three daughters to care for. What could I offer her? Nothing but my singular animal gift. My mind had degenerated to its present state, and my looks—once better than average—had gone the way of autumn.

I was not an attractive candidate as a stepfather to her daughters, who withdrew from me in horror once the excitement of the wedding faded and they realized cohabitation was inevitable. But we accommodated one another, and I like to believe they developed a fondness for me that was a little more than pity.

It was my suggestion that I move into the aviary as my senility became a problem. I would relay the details of this particular family discussion, but I can't recall them. And so, as my mind slipped, I moved into the aviary that Jane and her girls kept as a relic from days before their biological father was drowned. I was not averse in the least to the arrangement, as I adore birds and felt relief at the prospect of a life without pretense. The stepdaughters made me a cake, kissed my cheek, and their mother locked the gate with a wink. She returned that night (as she has most nights since) with a plate of fruit, wearing nothing but her robe and the scent of her bath.

These are our nights: the hymns of the retreating waves float disembodied in the cool salted cathedral air as we writhe in the sand, my jade stalk held fast, deep and pulsating between the gates of heaven, our rabid panting counterpointing the music of the sea as swarms of canaries careen wildly to and fro, tiny feathers loosened in their panicked flight floating in the thick air; the conures screech at the clouded moon; the cockatoos scream the garbled words my stepdaughters have taught them; the single black raven calls out in a mono-syllabic rasp, as if demanding calm. Hours later, we lie exhausted as shipwrecked sailors washed up on the cool sands of amnesia, eyes closed, dehydrated, our ears roaring softly with the chthonian motherhood that is our ocean. Once again, the agony has not come and I am content. The birds fall silent and there is only the eternal movement of the sea.

Is that your wife? The one who is waving? . . . Oh, I see. A fiancé. Congratulations! Ah, even from here I can see the sweet lift of her breasts with their berry-hard nipples longing to hiss at the sun and feed children. I can almost smell her. Go, go! If she comes up here to retrieve you, she may see me and then you would be without a woman. I'm just kidding, of course. Look at me. What use could any woman but Sweet Jane have for me?

But wait, let me give you some advice. Once married, you too, will experience some form of the aviary, and you will ask yourself, "What is the meaning of this?" And though you have not asked, my young friend, and I know you must go, I will answer that question: there is no meaning to the aviary. It is a home for birds.

~

As William sighed and closed his eyes, Ingenue smiled. His work was done and he would sleep soon. His pace had been slower today, almost as if he were composing rather than reciting from memory. But this approach seemed to suit the story.

Ingenue folded her computer and came to kneel beside him. She kissed his wrinkled neck, breathing the scent of him—a blend of leather and fermented jasmine—and whispered behind his ear, "That was lovely. So strange, so cruel, so sweet. I'll let you sleep now."

She placed her hand on his chest and he sank deeper into his chair, his head rolling to one side. He hardly seemed to breathe. She knew he was in the ocean where all his rivers ended, lower than all the lands of memory through which they had flowed to reach him.

She looked for Lily, but could not find her. Yet she was not disappointed, not really. Lily was the leader and must have things to do. She would see her again. She would love her again. The rooms in the house were deep in silence, sleeping with William; they shifted like the sea. She headed home to write.

It was raining and Ingenue had no umbrella. She dashed for

the porch and rang the bell. No answer. She tried the door. Locked. She was soaked—reports were that this was the most rain in a single week since 2020. She rang again. Nothing. She pounded. Still nothing.

Around the corner of the house was the large, multi-paned window with the wonderful view of the lake from the room where she and William worked. She would simply tap on the window. Of course he would not be able to see her, but at least he could alert the housekeeper that someone was outside. These sessions were scheduled, so *someone* must be expecting her. Lily had known about them, after all. But when Ingenue looked in through the window, his chair was empty and she stood alone in the brutal downpour, pelted by a billion droplets, so hot with rage the raindrops might hiss as they hit her skin.

Was she nothing? Considering the weather, could no one look out the window to see if she'd arrived? God knows there were no other visitors. The little weasel sitting in the guardhouse at the bottom of the hill had waved her through, so he must have called ahead.

She picked up a large decorative rock from the landscaping. That would get their attention—right through the window, a splash of broken glass shattering the warm serenity of this palatial prison of polyandry. That would bring the harem out.

Through the pouring, she chose her target: the pane in the center. As she took a few steps to her left and was about to take aim, she heard the voice.

"Hello! Hello! Over here!"

She dropped the rock and put her hand above her eyes, peering in the direction of the voice. Yes, there was a figure there, a woman—of course a woman—standing in the rain herself and waving her arms.

They stomped their feet on the porch, shaking themselves in

a canine fashion. Her savior was a plump woman with thick, brown, curly hair that held hundreds of sparkling droplets. But it was perfect. Ingenue had always wanted thick hair, glorious, glistening hair.

"I heard knocking, but by the time I got there, you'd escaped."

The woman's voice was nothing like Lily's, but rather an alto, almost as low as a man's, and there was an accent—no, not an accent, an inflection. She was not from this region.

"Let's get you undressed and into something easy and warm."

She pronounced something "some-ting," and why would one refer to clothing as "easy?" Clothes were many things but not easy. They were comfortable, they were glamorous, they were suitable, they were formal, they were informal—but when were they ever easy? Was English her second language? No, she must have a slight speech impediment, some sort of strange upbringing in a region where gene manipulation was legal—someplace before the holdover.

Then there was her hair, and her eyelashes, too: dark, soft, and dense. The eyebrows were also flawless, and perfectly arched. What must her pubic hair be like? Oh, this was embarrassing. One lesbian encounter with Lily and now she was admiring other women's eyebrows and wondering about their pubic hair.

Without another inflected word, the woman with the beautiful hair took Ingenue's hand and led her through a huge and immaculate old-style kitchen, down a long hallway with photographs of horses and geese, to a dressing room of sorts. There were racks of clothing, almost like a costume shop, and two floor-length mirrors.

The woman went to a drawer, and with a smile, motioned for Ingenue to come closer. Then, slowly, she opened the mahogany drawer. It came forth magically, as if on ball bearings—silently, and almost of its own accord—to reveal neatly folded gray-silver robes, of the same hue and texture as the clothes William had worn—was that on her last visit? She didn't know anymore. Events and stories had begun to run together like watercolors. Visits to the house were dreams, slow-motion versions of actual life, tinted with palpable shades of the uncanny, as if written by William.

The woman with perfect hair was undressing her now, and she let this happen. She'd expected it to happen, really, from the moment she'd seen the raindrops sparkling in that perfect hair.

Soon the woman was also naked, a vibrant bush of hair between her generous ivory thighs. The two women folded into each other, murmuring and whispering with the delicacy of strangers faced with a complex and inexorable pleasure, and when they had satisfied themselves like thirsty animals, the woman took one of the silver-gray robes and covered them both.

Ingenue ran her fingers through that glorious hair, buried her face in the smell of it, and fell sound asleep to dream of samurai warriors running loose in fields of purple cotton, laughing deliriously. Each time she came up for a moment of wakefulness during the night, she could feel the echoes of orgasm as they faded toward the new day— something she knew must come, would come, without her having interviewed William as scheduled.

The next session was a breakthrough.

"In my earliest memory," William said, "my grandfather is saying, 'Shall we to the cinema?' I'll never forget that. What did he mean by 'shall'? How strange. It was this peculiar use of the word that prompted me to start writing. I began using this word in notes I wrote to my imaginary friends. 'Shall we to the beach to swim?' Et cetera. It was so exciting. I guess I was about three or four."

"And you were already writing?"

"Well, I'm not sure you would call it that. I was making marks on paper and speaking, thinking I was writing the words. This became a lifelong habit."

"What kind of relationship did you have with your grandfather?"

"The imaginary kind. He was like a ghost. But I've written, as you know, many stories about grandfathers. All because of that word: shall. In fact, I have a grandfather story for you. It is in the hopper, so to speak, and while I had another I was going to dictate first, would you like to work on the grandfather story today?"

"I'd love that." She got up and kissed him on the cheek and gave him a little shoulder squeeze.

He beamed and sighed.

He was so manageable now that Lily showed her the way. And now that he was manageable, she was no longer in awe of him. Respect for him still swelled in her heart, but she'd released the girlish crush she'd arrived with. She had other crushes now.

She'd broken things off with The Idiot. Who got married these days, anyway? Marriage was a relic from her grandmother's day. Was that something Lily had told her? They corresponded now, though Lily was out of the region doing something official on William's behalf.

Ingenue was anxious, very anxious, to see her in person. The holographs did not do her justice, and she wanted to touch Lily again. In this house, and in all things related to this house, her sense of touch was excited—reclaimed— and that is what she loved about William, his writing, his presence, and his home. Touch.

William took a deep breath, exactly the kind a grandfather takes before telling a story. She wondered for an instant what his eyes actually looked like. She'd never seen them, shielded as they were by his dark glasses.

"This story is called, 'The Rapture Again.'"

My grandmother lay breathless in her hospital bed, the room lit with a chorus of flowers that made her greyness more intense. Her eyes twitched beneath thin-veined lids. I sat watching with my grandfather. He was nodding slightly, as if to answer some question he'd posed to himself in the solitude of his sorrow. A nurse with beautiful breasts—announced so perfectly in the professional sheath of her white uniform—arrived carrying a lunch of soft foods on a pink plastic tray. She peered down at my grandmother's delicate antique features and decided with a quick look that lunch was not what she needed.

When the nurse left, my grandfather turned to me, still nodding slightly. His hooded, almond-shaped eyes shone brightly above a straight, weathered beak. His hair was impeccably placed, but tufts of gray whiskers sprung from his large ears. His mother had been French and wealthy, his father Chinese and intelligent. He was American, a retired professor of Chinese history.

But it was my grandmother I remembered warmly from the childhood summers I'd spent in their home in Oregon. She was a hugger, my grandmother, and the pride she took in my smallest accomplishment was broadcast to the world— waiters, the mailman, cashiers at the supermarket—none were immune to her earnest descriptions of my intelligence and creativity.

By contrast, I had little interest in my grandfather besides a vague curiosity I developed about him as an adult. I was happy to leave him to his books and endless cups of tea. It was his wife I loved.

My grandfather cleared his throat and said, "That people can speak to each other in different languages and reach a misunderstanding so precise as to stagger the imagination is nothing new. What is remarkable is that people who never see each other can have families without ever having touched one another."

It was not the content of these sentences that stunned me, for he had always been a man of peculiar ideas and odd pronouncements. I had sat at his dinner table on holidays and other significant occasions for much of my life, and was used to his non sequitur regressions into Chinese history and his infantile metaphysical anecdotes. What stunned me was that he adopted, in his statement, my own stilted sentence structure. He continued.

"The mechanics are not important. The mechanics have never been important. The mechanics never will be important. The mechanics of how two people can never touch or see each other as you and I physically see each other, and yet still produce a family, are unknowable, and so for the purposes of our story they do not exist. They never will exist. In fact, our memory of having spoken of them will disappear. It soon will not have existed, nor will it ever exist. Thus, mechanics are verified. There is no need to speak further of them."

Could he be mimicking me? Did he know how sensitive I was about the "perfunctory oddness" of my speaking style? If so, why would he choose to mock me here, at the water's edge of death, where his wife of fifty-five years was about to float away?

"I have had such a relationship. I have raised such a family. You see, long ago I adopted the point of view that if I saw a beautiful woman I wanted, I was actually looking into the future. As a historian, I knew that the past does not exist. There is only the present and its potential. And potential, of course, is infinite. History is created twice: when it is written and when it is read. It is a form of fiction, a sort of theater for the mind. Here is the correct picture. A bird flies through an endless sky. That bird is the present moment and the sky is the Land of Time, or potential, through which the bird believes he is flying. I learned these things from studying the past that does not exist. My route to knowledge was indirect."

His words had the confident clarity only the insane or senile can muster. Had grief galvanized him into a telepathic discontinuity, allowing him to mimic me and dream out loud at the same time?

"You see, no matter how much a man loves his wife, he will become bored with her. Unavoidable. True one hundred times out of one hundred times. Never varies. And if a man says otherwise, he is a liar. Of course, a woman becomes bored with her husband too, but that is not my concern. In a good marriage these things are kept private. Privacy is the key to a long marriage. One should marry with both eyes open and then immediately close one eye so as not to see what should be private and hidden in his or her mate. Too much intimacy will destroy a marriage as quickly as too little of it."

I was staring at him now, hoping he would sense my alarm, though I had a desire to hear more.

"Naturally, marriage being the necessary partnership that it is, I kept my mouth shut. I did not want to lose my wife. But I began to imagine another woman while I made love to your grandmother."

I made the most disapproving face I could manage, but, misunderstanding my intent, his eyes brightened and he pushed on.

"I imagined her exactly as I pleased. With memory and imagination, I carved a woman without flaw from living ether. If there was something I liked about a girl I'd slept with as a boy—perhaps a subtle coloration of the nipples—then I included this in my creation. Every texture and firmness I desired was brought to perfection."

Following my grandfather's hand in a gesture he made to illustrate the word "firmness," I noticed that there was a cluster of ants on the cuff of his tweed sports coat. Looking more closely I saw that there were several dozen ants on his sleeve. They formed an energetic tributary snaking itself to his shoulder, under his arm and into the pocket of his coat. The old guy probably had a piece of candy or half a bagel in his pocket. Being without his wife these past months—his nurse and housekeeper all these years—he'd probably let the house go and the vigorous little soldiers had moved in. Who knew how long the linty coat had lay on a chair in the kitchen, its stale treasure providing a feast for the tiny workers slowly encroaching on their home. Oblivious to the ants, he continued.

"I literally pumped life into my vision. With every copulatory stroke of my phallic utensil, I painted, groomed, and exhumed her from the invisibility of the nonexistent. I became an erotic god garnering the forces of creation from ancient alchemical institutions. I moved beyond history! I moved from within the true constructs of boundless time."

The old fart had achieved a highly agitated state. Saliva flew as he spoke, and I noticed his teeth were yellowed and filmy, with small bits of past meals wedged in the gaps. Bristling with his re-creation, his eyes sparkled.

"Of course, it took years. One does not construct a goddess in an afternoon. Each time I made love to your grandmother, I brought up the vision and fed it the juices of my soul. You see, boy, in a way you are a result of my goddess. It was through her that I became inspired enough to continue the procreative procedures that led to your mother's birth, and thus your own, for I was never terribly fond of the mechanics involved. True, I was always potent enough, but such rudimentary grinding and slashing would never have held my interest. I needed grist for a cosmic mill. I wanted to people the earth from all directions."

The ants had encroached upon the octogenarian's leathered neck and were exploring the road map of wrinkles leading to his large ears. In a normal state of mind, he would have felt them marching, but entranced as he was, he launched into the next phase of his narrative before I could warn him of the invasion.

"By the time I was thirty she was quite real. I would turn her over and over like a hologram in my mind's eye as your grandmother and I hammered away at each other. But don't think for a moment, young man, that I ever neglected your grandmother. I was a dutiful and dedicated lover, always making sure I pleased her in the way she desired. She told me many times how much she appreciated this. Of course, she never knew of my project, my creation, my secret other-worldly joy in the Land of Time."

He paused a moment, eyes misted, lips tremulous and crusted. For the first time, I noticed an odd nobility about my grandfather, an absurd dignity that resided in his anachronistic manners and the gnarled hands that stuck from his cuffs like tree roots exposed by floods and wind.

"When my creation first spoke to me, I was moved to tears. Your grandmother and I were on vacation on the coast. We had a lovely dinner: lobster and an excellent Riesling. Then we returned to our room to make love. The window was open. There was a cool sea breeze. We lay on top of the sheets, tasting the air with our bodies, our minds half asleep with wine. When we fell to making love, my creation appeared and, of course, I was making love to her, as well. Quite abruptly, my goddess said, 'We will need a home if we are to continue.'"

My grandfather lifted his eyebrows and stared at me—fully expecting me, I'm sure, to be as enthralled with this recollection as he. But I was more concerned with the ants. They seemed to have disappeared, or at least retreated, beneath the cover of his clothing, or somehow into the recesses of the rugged geography of his body—perhaps even into the safety of his veined ears.

"Though moved, I was not so stunned at the time. As I mentioned, I was a bit tipsy. But the next day, I reflected on the absolute reality and the implication of her words. The horrifying thing was that she had spoken completely of her own accord. Until this time she had been malleable. Her very existence belonged to me and was, in fact, my creation. I formed her—from her green eyes, to her perfect toenails, to her rose-colored nipples. She was mine. But now she was speaking of her own will. Terrified, I decided to abandon the project immediately."

Could I have imagined the ants? Was I becoming as hallucinatory as the old man? Perhaps, for reasons unfathomable, they had all proceeded to the other side of his body where I could not see them.

"But it was of no use," he continued. "The moment your grandmother and I were joined in a genital embrace, the rapture appeared again! This time I knew there was no denying her. For one thing, she was unbelievably beautiful. And, quite naturally, since I had created her—or at least I thought I had—within the womb of my own aesthetic, she knew my susceptibilities all too well. Secondly, she emanated a sense of purpose as palpable as your grandmother's body moving beneath me."

I must confess that I had been drawn into his story, despite my disgust and concern about the ants. What did I care? There was nothing I could do now to save my grandmother from his eccentricity. She was departing. Naturally, he was lonely and needed to unburden his heart of its wild and guilty luggage. Besides, I'd never heard a story quite like it.

"She persisted, and as we made love, she laid plans in my ear, telling me where she wanted us to live and how long it would take her to create such a place. Now, until this time, I had not spoken to her. There had been only telepathic and erotic communication—intercourse, but no discourse. But what could I do? What began as a figment of my imagination was now an active entity in my environment. If I did not speak to her, if I did not set boundaries, how could I know the limits of her intrusive powers?"

The nurse with the delightful breasts returned with a cup

of tea for my grandfather. As providing tea for the relatives of the afflicted was not a typical duty of nurses, I assumed she had grown fond of the old fellow keeping vigil at the bedside of his dying wife. She had no idea he was at this moment relating a tale of infidelity that transcended the boundaries of reality. She brought no tea for me, but what did that matter? I let my eyes rest gently on her breasts, barely contained by the white starched medical costume. With a faint smile, she bent at the waist to present the old man with the steaming cup. She patted his shoulder (no sign of the ants) and left the room with a sigh. My grandfather continued.

"I spoke to the creation, very gently: 'Why are you talking all of a sudden?' But it was your grandmother who responded, 'I didn't say anything, honey, but I'm about to come.' In the midst of your grandmother's orgasm, I realized that this was no fantasy; I truly inhabited two women. Even as my wife squirmed in the fading contractions of climax, I spoke to my darling, this woman of another world—silently now, in my mind—about how I was unwilling to continue this infidelity with her."

With a motion of my hand I urged him to drink his tea. I didn't want the nurse's kindness to be wasted. As he took a long sip, I felt a silent communion with the nurse. I was beginning to like the old guy myself, despite my early feelings of repugnance. Still, I felt the orgasms of one's grandmother needn't be discussed within earshot of her deathbed.

"But it was absolutely to no avail," he went on, "for once I began to speak to her, I came to occupy her world. As I drifted off to sleep each night, she was with me—in what we would technically have to call dreams, because I was asleep to this world. We were together, walking naked in the Land of Time where I would be her husband in an orthodoxy whose rules I could never fathom."

He leaned back for a moment, slurping the tea as if it were some prescribed invalid broth he must consume before speaking another word. Visiting hours had drawn to a close and the lights in the hall had been dimmed. I suspected we were the only visitors left—due, I was sure, to the nurse's kindness. My grandfather placed the empty teacup and its saucer on the floor before him, then massaged the wrinkled skin beneath his chin with his thumb and forefinger, nodding slowly, as if in response to something only he could hear.

"Henceforth, I was always with her. It didn't matter what I was doing. I could be in my office studying the *I Ching* or going for a walk with your grandmother. It no longer mattered. I was living with her. Many mornings I awoke with clear memories of the past few days. How we had dug a little pond behind the house or made a bear out of the small marshmallows she sometimes pulled from her body. Little domestic notes from that world. And I confess—I have nothing to lose now—that I grew to love her deeply. It was a nice life—always naked, always flowing and changing in a world I could not control. Still, there was no coital activity unless I was involved with your grandmother. Only then did we make love. It was a point of intersection."

He turned and looked at me, a faint smile softening the cragged planes of his face. I nodded in return, questions forming behind my eyes, but he was off again.

"Well, my darling conceived and we had a daughter. The whole thing happened in what to us might be a few minutes, or maybe years. I don't know. The mechanics are incomprehensible, but I'm trying to give you a clear picture; it will be important to you. That night your grandmother and I made love in the pantry. It was a freakish thing. She was on her tiptoes reaching for the baking powder and I was standing behind her. I embraced her from behind and soon the door was shut, she was on her knees, and I was grasping those delicate naked hips as if I were clinging to a galloping horse. I rode and plunged with all the smells of food and spices of our fully-stocked pantry rushing in and out of my nostrils.

Of course, my darling was there, too, and a few weeks later, while I was sitting on the back porch finishing an explosively ripe plum, I remembered the birth. This is what I recall: as your grandmother and I finished on the pantry floor, my darling, in the Land of Time, took the seed inside her with a conscious grasp. She then lay back on a sort of maroon colored platform, as I remember. I say platform because there is no way to really relate the architectural details of that world. She opened those long beautiful legs that I had created. But the really wondrous thing was that I seemed to be able to see inside her belly."

There was a slight rustling to my left. I realized, with a covert glance, that the nurse was standing quietly, with her hands folded in front of her, a few feet from the foot of the bed.

"I saw the seed bravely approach the egg and engage, consumed in the instant before my daughter began to form. Her mother's belly swelled, growing moment by moment as her legs opened even wider and sweat glazed her skin. The door of her womb began changing colors in harmony with some kind of drum that was distantly marking time. The labia formed two separate hands. It was as if someone was pulling on gloves from within her body. There was a wonderful animal aroma. Blood trickled from between the hands of the vagina, and then, in a moment, there came a rush of myriad fluids. The huge mound of her abdomen began to throb and pound, and she screamed, "I'm coming," as a river of green, yellow, black, and violet poured from between her legs. Soon I was calf-deep in it. It started to rain and there was a tremendous thrashing about. I reached out to assist, but I was helpless in this hurricane of body fluids—then suddenly was crushed under an oceanic amniotic wave. I could hardly breathe. I was drowning in this birth! I remember thinking, 'How could I have created this? How did I get here?' But my moment of panic passed. Suddenly, miraculously, it was calm again.

With the liquids now speeding toward the sky, I saw my baby emerge, mottled, head-first, as the vagina hands helped her through, until she stood before me smiling and flapping her arms as if trying to fly. 'I'm here,' she said."

I had been listening so intently, and he had been telling the story so intently, that neither of us noticed my grandmother sitting up in bed staring at us. I had never before seen the smile that came across her small face. She seemed, in that instant, like a different person, imbued with a personality familiar to me, but unplaceable.

The nurse moved to the side of the bed and held out her hand for my grandmother, who took it for a moment and then reclined with a sigh. The nurse indicated that it was time for us to leave with a pleasant nod toward the door, so we stood. My grandfather approached the bed, bent and gently kissed his motionless wife's pale, still lips. The nurse smiled as if to acknowledge the sweetness of the scene, placing her left hand on her right breast—beneath which, no doubt, beat the warm heart of a true professional nurse. As my grandfather passed her on his way to the door, she patted him again on the shoulder.

In the hall, as we stood for a moment, my grandfather grasped my elbow with his gnarled fingers and whispered harshly into my ear.

"Those were not your grandmother's eyes! She was looking in from somewhere else. But listen to me please. I want you to find the daughter I had with my Darling of the Land of Time. I want you to find her and marry her. Don't worry that she is, by the rules of this world, your aunt. This is not a thing of blood. Please find her, take care of her and be a good husband to her. She is alone. Please . . ."

I held up my finger with the wedding band to remind him I was married, but he brushed my hand away.

"The mechanics do not exist. Please, for everyone's sake, find her. Create her if you must. Indulge me. I am your grandfather!"

My ear was wet from the blast of his demand. I strained to disengage my arm from his talons and opened my mouth, finally willing to voice my disgust or at least reel him in a bit—remind him that his wife was dying and that we should be concerned about nothing but her peaceful passage—but before I could speak, the door to my grandmother's room opened.

The nurse, her face radiant with empathy, motioned us inside. My grandmother was leaving this world. My grandfather's arthritic claw went limp and we stood frozen between worlds for a moment. I knew he was right. The mechanics do not exist. His shoulders slumped and a shudder of resignation passed through his body.

I followed him through the door to say goodbye to my grandmother, my course in life now set, an unwilling initiate in a futile family quest.

He sobbed now, spine-rattling convulsions of grief for the woman he loved.

Oblivious to his sorrow, the ants had resumed their march toward his mahogany ear.

~

"That was magnificent, William!"

He was exhausted, she could tell. He was not panting, but his breathing was a bit deep, as if he'd used more air than he owned. She knelt before him and held his hands. "You sleep now. That was a brilliant story. And all from that one word. I shall never think of 'shall' in the same way." But the joke was lost on him. He was asleep. She ran her hand up and down his leg. On the third time she went further north and felt the limp body of his manhood sheathed in the gray-silver pants, as lifeless as an overripe zucchini.

Today the pregnant housekeeper showed her out. She

didn't want to leave, but she'd learned not to press herself into the affairs of the house. What happened would happen. Surprises should not be forced or explicated. But she did ask the pregnant housekeeper, "Do you have a nursery here? I thought I heard babies crying one time." The woman shook her head as if she did not understand, then took Ingenue's hand with both of her own and placed it on the half globe of her belly. She felt the baby move beneath the woman's skin. She kissed the woman softly on the lips and left.

Ingenue decided at the beginning of her next visit to remain standing. Rather than taking dictation, she pressed the record button on her computer and left it on a nearby table. She didn't even unfold it. Now she could walk around the room, move close to him, back away—she could zoom in or out to touch his shoulder or give him a kiss on the top of his head to keep him talking. It worked like a charm.

She breathed deeply as she moved around the room, smelling the lovely mahogany and lilac scent of the mansion, feeling completely a part of the place. In this feeling of belonging, there was knowledge and resolution. She knew that she, too, was being impregnated: today, finally, he began to give her the actual details of his youth.

"I never knew my place," he said, "and so I looked inward. But I did not look inward intellectually or spiritually. I looked inward physically. I would sprint full-speed across the meadow behind my grandmother's house, then slip into the quietest room in the house to listen to my thunderous heartbeat until it became too calm and quiet to hear. Naturally, I touched myself everywhere. Not just genitally. I took long baths with my eyes closed, trying to hear what my skin was saying. I stood naked in the meadow at midnight with my mouth stuffed full of pomegranate seeds, chewing slowly as the wild juice ran down my chin, throat, and chest. And while I lived in a kingdom of touch, I lived alone.

"Strangely, I was aroused from early on by the rituals of the Catholic Church. The mahogany Christ in cruciform, the praying priests in their scarlet-trimmed robes, the candles, the chanted prayers, the smoke of incense rising into the universe of the high ceilinged church. Holy water, holy this, holy that. Taking the body of Christ onto the tongue, drinking blood turned to wine. Then there were all the women, so well-dressed: young ones with pert breasts and bored expressions, matronly ones with absurd red lipstick, women who sat in the child room breastfeeding their babies. Mass was an erotic wonder to me. The music, the sin, the redemption, God, the flesh, and the world of smells: incense, perfume, the aftershave of the freshly shaved men, the powdered babies, the spring air wafting in from the open doors at the rear of the theater. There I lost my virginity—not of the body, but of the head and mind. I was swept away.

"Later, of course, I figured out what their message really was and I lost interest. By that time Mass had been replaced by girls, fistfighting, smoking stolen cigarettes, and reading books. Still, I owe a great deal to the Catholic Church."

She was pleased, but not inordinately so. The story about the aviary—her favorite—was actually more interesting than these biographical tidbits. She did believe the pomegranate juice and the Catholic Church were real memories, and she could certainly weave this into some kind of biographical through-line to help a reader interested in his books understand the antecedents. But why would anyone want to bother with the everyday antecedents when they could go instead to "The Aviary"?

"You knew, William, that I would eventually see the actuality of your life to be far less fascinating that what you have written, didn't you?"

William took off his dark glasses and looked directly into her eyes. He was not blind. Her heart leapt. Of course he was not blind. His gaze was piercing, direct, and sweet. She'd been betrayed. Seduced. "Yes, I did. That is why I was blind to you. And that is why I wrote you."

She could hear her own heart pounding now. "But you didn't write me. I wrote you. Remember? I wrote and asked you—"

"I don't mean 'wrote *to* you,'" he countered, his seeing eyes holding her pinned in midair, "I mean, 'the way I *wrote* you.'"

"What?"

"We both know that I could see the whole time. We both know that your existence is one I created. There is no actual world. Even though you are simply a character of mine, you know that everything is fiction. In a universe of infinite possibility, there is no discovery, there is only creation."

"Well, that's just—are you saying I don't exist to you, except as a character in your imagination?"

"You know it's true," he said, finally blinking. "We are in this story together and that is all. Beyond its reading and writing, you don't exist. Only when you come here are you real."

"Oh, really?" She felt dizzy now and backed herself down into a chair.

"For example, The Idiot you told me you were going to marry."

"I never told you about The Idiot."

"Exactly. How would I know, then? I know because I wrote it."

"William, you did not write me."

"Then tell me about The Idiot."

"Well, he's an idiot."

"What does he look like?"

"Like an idiot."

"Yes," he said. "You only know of him what I wrote, which is very little. You only know of yourself what I wrote. Your work colleagues, your idiot, your playing second base on your high school softball team. These are things I wrote, and, as a result, are the only things you know about yourself. Tell me something new. What was your father's name?"

She opened her mouth, but nothing came. She stared at him, the old man with the young man's seeing eyes, and she had no idea who she was. There was no father.

"That's right," he said. "There was no father."

If what he was saying were true, then she'd originated in this house, like Lily, the pregnant woman, and the one with the beautiful hair. Yet Ingenue felt sure she was real—what he'd said could not be true. She tried to remember something beyond the interviews, the mansion, and the memories William had written for her. There was nothing. A curtain fell. It was a death—the death of she who had never lived. Yet the memories she did have were vivid and precious: the ones, for example, of lying in bed with William's books as a young girl. These memories were as clear as vivid dreams, like movies she could play over and over. But there was no father down the hall in a bedroom with her mother. There was, in fact, no mother. Finally, there was no house.

All her interviews with William had been written by him. But they were real to her. They were her character and she was no less real for being unreal. She was here. "Does this mean I can no longer leave the house?" she asked.

"Do you want to leave? Where would you go?"

"But wait!" She lurched forward. "I have a car in the driveway. I drive down that long driveway with the big stones on the sides of it and I pass through the gate with the watch hut and the hunched man who knows me—he will tell you I am real—and then I leave!"

"Where do you go?"

"I. . . I have some bits of. . . a life. . . but they just float there. My job, my apartment. But they are. . ."

"Half-written?"

"Yes."

He had closed his eyes now and his whole posture had changed. He was more stooped, older perhaps, and smaller. She knew he was blind again. He patted his lap, searching for his sunglasses. They'd fallen to the floor. She picked them up and slipped them on for him. He kept his eyes closed, not wanting her to see what they looked like when he was written blind. So vain he was.

"But we must blind ourselves to this truth," he said weakly.

"We must," she said, feeling suddenly more herself. In fact, she felt strong and professional—she was a powerful inhabitant of her character. She knew what to do and how to do it.

"A few more questions, my darling, then I'll let you sleep."

"Certainly, you deserve the best." He sat up a little straighter, preparing himself.

"So, there is a nursery?"

"There is."

"And the children are real?"

"As real as you and I sitting here."

"And the world outside the house in the year 2045. That, too, is real?"

"As real as the day and night we inhabit."

"And what becomes of the babies, William?"

"They grow up, of course, and live their lives."

"But where will they go? What will they do?"

I don't know. I will be dead by then. But you may see them and know how things turn out."

"So, really then, the fact that everything is fiction changes nothing."

"True. And what you will write of me in your book— that is true, too. The world is not made of facts. The true world is far too immense and mysterious for facts. They are simply the womb through which truth comes."

"And you know then that I am an actual person, with a real life as complete as yours in my own universe. I'm just as complete as you. Nothing more, nothing less."

"So it is written," he said smiling. "Absolutely true."

She paused for a few moments, staring out the window at the afternoon light and the shadows beneath the trees. When she looked back to him, he was sleeping soundly.

Lily Cordovia was waiting for her in the parlor. As glad as Ingenue was to see her, she was disturbed by the fact that she now knew her last name. How did she know that? Was it being written?

Lily nodded when she asked if her last name was, indeed, Cordovia. "Didn't you know that?"

"Not until now," she said, looking up into Lily's green eyes.

With the tall woman's baby clearly growing, the length of her trunk was thicker, her breasts in full bloom. And while they sat across from each other in an almost matronly fashion, Lily seemed more approachable. Even with her austerity abated, and the royalty of her green eyes now almost pastoral, her smile was still as seductive as ever, and soon she and Ingenue were on the same couch. Lily caressed Ingenue's neck softly as they spoke.

"He told me that I am written," Ingenue said. "That he has written me. Then, when I tried to recall my life outside the house, I could not. Even now I cannot remember my father's name."

Lily sighed and kissed her forehead. "Did he take off his glasses and pretend to see?"

"Yes! He *can* see. He looked directly into my eyes and spoke to me. Everything he said was irrefutable."

"No, my dear, he cannot see. He is blind as a bat in formaldehyde. It was his voice, his mesmerism, and his talent for seduction that erased parts of your memory. He has done that to us all at some point. It's one more of his tricks, old coyote that he is. Your memory is coming back. You can remember your father's name now."

"It was Theodore, of course. And The Idiot is real. Jesus Christ! How can he do that? Did he hypnotize me?"

"Hypnotism might be the wrong word. He is a sort of shamanic con man. Don't worry, you're immune now that you've experienced it. He is a special man and we love him, but we can't be swayed by him more than once. And we must fulfill our function."

"Which is?"

"To have his children. To fulfill old mysteries as we were chosen to do."

"Chosen by whom?"

"Well, that is a much more difficult question. Yet we follow out of duty, even as the tradition grows weaker. You, for example, come here with no knowledge of why or how, proving how weak the tradition is becoming. No offense."

"Lily, what are you talking about?"

"Of course, when people no longer read, it will all be gone. We all read, don't we? Every one of us. We read seriously. And that is the vanishing magic."

"That's why I came. To be sure he is not forgotten. What people read now is not really reading. It's just information and confession. We can't let this slip away. But this harem— what is that about?"

Lily laughed. "There is no harem. We are an army. That lovely old geezer is a brilliant writer, and we are keeping that alive, genetically. This happy mission is not just literary; sensuality is dying along with literature. We are losing our ability to immerse ourselves. We artificially inseminate and take our genetic artifice for granted. Out of our control. But this army—our army—takes a stand in nature, with William. Our inseminating is not artificial."

"You mean you have sex with him."

"Of course."

"To have his children."

"Yes."

"I can't imagine. I love him, but I don't think I could do that."

Lily laughed her beautiful high laugh and, moved by that laugh, Ingenue put her hand on the tall woman's knee and slid it up between her thighs.

Being a member of an army—Lily, the others, the babies—it aroused her. It was so much more interesting than her job or The Idiot. She did not care that she had been mesmerized. What did it matter? This was exciting. This was living literature.

"But wait," she said. "How did he make his eyes come alive like that? How did he look into my eyes and speak to me with that energy, that youth?"

"He wrote it," Lily giggled, her thighs opening. Kneeling before this tall woman, Ingenue was certain that the memory of the velvet wetness she was about taste could never be taken from her, not even by William. Lily's hips rose, the delta of magic, honey, and babies opening to the phallic tongue. The kiss of the soul surrendering to duty.

"Once one masters an art," William said, pointing toward the ceiling, "the possibilities are endless."

"But is mastery an ongoing process?"

"Well, you keep evolving once you attain it, but mastery itself is simply a point at which your restraints are all undone. You have weaknesses, but they no longer confine you. They are part of your technique and you use them. One more color on your palette. You are no longer dependent on the world for material—or on your own imagination. You simply follow the language. You step into the arena, sword in hand, and wait for the Mirror Beast."

"The mirror beast?"

"Yes, and capitalize the M and the B when you write it.

Mirror Beast.

"But what is it?"

"It is whatever it approaches. Whatever approaches, you shatter lovingly. You don't have to worry about all the revisions. You pick up the shattered Mirror Beast and reconstruct the world, letting the language lead you."

"And if people can't relate to it?"

"Caring about what others think is what you do when you are striving for mastery. You make yourself an apprentice, or a slave, to the opinions of others. You make them into a mirror and stand before it, constantly judging yourself by what they think. The master only deals with the Mirror Beast."

"What is the difference between the mirror and the Mirror Beast?"

"The Mirror Beast is the soul of the artist, not the soul of others."

"So you are shattering your own soul?"

"To shatter someone else's would be a violation, wouldn't it?"

She pulled a chair close and, facing him, stared directly into the dark-lensed pools of his shielded eyes. "Last time you said you wrote me and my life, and now you tell me I am part of the Mirror Beast that you must slay in an imaginary arena. You can't have it both ways."

He sighed. "You want to rearrange things, dear, but we can't do that."

"What do you mean, rearrange?"

"When you smell something, just as I can smell you right now—your shampoo, the faint hint of that incense you burn in your bedroom, the slightly metallic smell that tells me you started your period recently—that is happening in the present. Whatever we said to each other before is past. We can't rearrange things. We can't make that happen again."

"Ah-ha!" She stood bolt upright. "You smell these

things? I came into the room with these smells, so how could you have written them?"

"The past is written by the present. As I told you how you smelled, I was authoring your memory."

"Okay, that's it. We are not going any further in this direction. What has happened to you? This makes no sense."

"It is ineffable," he acknowledged. "But I want you to understand this one thing. You said when you came that you did not want me to be forgotten. Well, I wish to be forgotten and that is what death brings us, forgetfulness. For if we cannot remember ourselves, how can others remember us?"

He was silent for a moment, and then a tear ran down his cheek. "Everything is possible when you can follow the language. We live in a semantically-created world. Well, I do. And I think you do, too. You, the character, are a semantic pattern, a history of words." He sighed deeply and wiped away the tear. "But I cannot follow the language fully anymore. I have no story for you today. I believe I am done."

She sprung to his side. "No—you are not done. I'm sorry I badgered you. You sleep now. I'll come back. No more pestering you about these things. Please, just relax." On her knees next to the chair, she pulled him close. He was soft and pliable. A menstrual cramp as strong as the kick of a child moved in her womb.

Ingenue did not visit the house for three weeks. William was ill, she'd been told, and she was busy putting together a new version of his biography. It would consist of an introduction by Lily Cordovia, two of her own essays on William's work, followed by his stories: "Buoyant," "The Runner," "In the Aviary," "The Rapture Again," and finally, the story she was in, "Pollen." This, she'd decided, was the best approach.

Then Lily called and asked about her cycle. She checked and found she was fertile for the next forty-eight hours.

"William is dying. You have to come now. This is your

chance."

Ingenue folded her computer, put it in her purse, and left the office. She didn't bother to stop at the apartment. There was nothing there she wanted and everything she needed would be provided.

She drove to her new home, attacking the rain-slick uphill curves with resolve. She was going home to the women she loved, to William, and to her child soon to come. The man in the guardhouse welcomed her with his dwarfish salute.

The gravel crunched like fresh snow beneath her feet. A breeze flung the light rain into her eyes and the warm golden light poured from the front window. Her vision prismed by the rain, she glimpsed him there in his chair, the king ensconced in his sunken leather throne: his dark-shaded eyes, his silver hair, his smooth skin and his gray clothing.

He was looking at her. Just as she'd thought, he could see all along. He couldn't possibly die. Her heart lurched out to him and she ran toward the light, but when she had blinked away her tears, she saw clearly that the chair was empty behind the droplet-splattered window.

A boy opened the door—at least she thought it was a boy for a moment.

Trim and muscular, with a short haircut, the person greeted her with a bit of a smirk. "They are waiting for you. All the girly girls are in the nursery cooing over the babies. They sound like a bunch of whales, making those high sounds women make when they see soft, helpless, little things."

The person looked Ingenue up and down, and then pointed down the hall.

The Rain Woman with the beautiful hair waited at the end of the hall, smiling. "Do you want to see the nursery before we go?"

"Go where?"

"To the Viridian Room."

As Ingenue allowed the Rain Woman to lead her toward the nursery, panic gripped her for an instant. She was going to have a baby! A body was going to grow like an alien inside her, then force its way out. She would be inhabited.

Sensing her panic, the Rain Woman pulled her close for a moment and Ingenue smelled her flawless hair, an aromatic mass of cascades and color.

Then they were in the nursery and the cooing soothed her. The scents of baby's breath and lactation filled the candlelit room like incense.

Across the room, a group of women huddled around a low bed. It was the housekeeper, feeding her newborn child. The cooing women kissed the baby's head, hands, and tiny feet. The infant's new lips pursed and pulled, drawing the first fluids of life from the housekeeper's bursting breast, her free nipple spraying tiny lines of milk into the air with the rhythm of the child's sucking.

Tears came to Ingenue's eyes.

Yet another mother, a young woman with grayish skin and the pink eyes of an albino, motioned her closer.

She knelt and leaned in, pressing her face for a few moments gently into the baby's soft round torso. The smell was wondrous: new, fresh, innocent. The Rain Woman tapped her on the shoulder and whispered, "We have to hurry."

The cathedral ceiling of the Viridian Room swirled with birds in orchestral pursuit of one another, their various voices blooming in all directions, an auditory bouquet flung at high mahogany beams.

Sunk deep in the green pillows, Ingenue let her mind race with thoughts of the child who would someday suckle her breasts just as the Rain Woman did now. But those thoughts were quickly washed away. Other women had arrived, and they moved in concert. The choreography of their touch enclosed her in a womb—protective, urgent, purposefully moving her toward the inward and opiate convulsion that conquered everything, leaving her trembling and receptive.

When she was prepared past satiation, they took her to the Round Room at the top of the stone stairway. She was at the center of the group, and when they opened the thick door at the top landing, every hand pushed her gently across the threshold.

There, beneath amber lights, William was laid out naked on a small platform bed, hooked to a maze of medical machinery—his purpled, medically-enhanced erection in dramatic contrast to his pale, thin body. It was a slender lingam with a large head and resembled a question mark. His eyes were closed.

A nurse in a uniform from another century knelt massaging his scalp, as yet another woman—slender, dark-skinned and naked—held his hand.

Lily led Ingenue to the platform as the soft sound of a distant ocean lapped over her.

The other women helped her up to straddle him. She marveled again at his erection. Even chemically induced, it was at once humble and magnificent. He seemed to barely be breathing.

She squatted, easing herself down slowly so his entrance into her was gentle and caused him no pain. He opened his eyes, blind in the face of death. She began to move, pulling, contracting, and coercing as the nurse sang a simple song:

> *"What do we do*
> *When we are through with love*
> *And love is through with us*
> *Do we drown in lust*
> *Do we simply rust*
> *What do we do*

When love is through with us?"

"He's going now," Lily whispered, and Ingenue could feel that he was.

A soft shudder traveled up his body and he gave up his last seed inside her.

Ingenue looked down and saw William's lips moving, but she couldn't hear him. She bent forward and put her ear next to his mouth as he repeated his final words.

"I am pollen."